Look to the Sky

by
Jerry DeBruin
and
Don Murad

illustrated by Rochana Junkasem

Cover by Jeff Van Kanegan

Copyright © Good Apple, Inc., 1988

GOOD APPLE, INC.
BOX 299
CARTHAGE, IL 62321-0299

2360105

Copyright © Good Apple, Inc., 1988
ISBN No. 0-86653-440-7
Printing No. 987654321

GOOD APPLE, INC.
BOX 299
CARTHAGE, IL 62321-0299

INSPIRATION

"I'd Like to Roller-Skate on the Moon"

Words and Music by Doug Nichol*

Some people don't know how to dream at all.
     They won't let their minds roll on.
Well one of these days they'd better wake up
   or their chances will all be gone.
We only have one chance at life
     At least that's what they say,
So take my hand before it gets too late.
     We'd better get started today. —

(chorus)

I'd like to roller-skate on the moon.
     I'd like to tap-dance on a star,
I'd like to jump up and down on the fluffy clouds
     and spend a day on Mars.
I'd like to climb up on a rainbow
     and slide into the pot of gold.
Come along with me let's give it a try
     before we get too old.—

Take all your money and give it away.
     You won't need it any more.
Stuff all your worries in a closet.
     Then shut and lock the door.
Don't take time to pack your bag—
     Come just as you are.
Take my hand before it gets too late,
     'cause you and I could go far.—

(chorus)

I'd like to roller-skate on the moon
     I'd like to tap-dance on a star,
I'd like to jump up and down on the fluffy clouds
     and spend a day on Mars.
I'd like to climb up on a rainbow
     and slide into the pot of gold.
Come along with me let's give it a try
     before we get too old.—

*Used with permission.

iii

TABLE OF CONTENTS

INTRODUCTION: A Note to Teachers and Parents

Dear Friends,

Thank you for the many kind comments about my previous eighteen books—*Touching and Teaching Metrics Series; Cardboard Carpentry; Creative, Hands-On Science Experiences;* the *Young Scientists Explore Series—Intermediate;* and *Scientists Around the World*—all published by Good Apple, Inc., from 1977 to 1987.

Part of the fun in writing books for Good Apple this past decade has been the opportunity to meet new people and subsequently introduce them to writing science books for parents, teachers and youngsters. Such was the case with Linda Penn, a personal friend and author of the highly successful *Young Scientists Explore Series—Primary.*

This book, *Look to the Sky,* features the introduction of a new writer, Don Murad, a highly successful secondary school physics and astronomy teacher. My relationship with Don began eight years ago and continues to grow each day because of our mutual interest in *Look to the Sky.* It is my hope that you will welcome Don to the field of science writing as much as you welcomed Linda and her works in the past.

From all of us we hope that the information and activities in *Look to the Sky* will touch many minds, hearts and hands and that much personal growth will be experienced by all who use *Look to the Sky.* Keep in touch. Let us know how you are doing. It is always good to hear from you. Until then, best wishes for your continued growth as a scientist and as a complete human being.

Sincerely,

Jerry DeBruin

OVERVIEW: How to Use This Book

We hope that you as parents and teachers will enjoy using *Look to the Sky*. This 4-12 guide features materials and activities that are interdisciplinary in scope, which means they are easily integrated into other academic disciplines. Part One, HOW TO BEGIN TO LOOK TO THE SKY, first encourages you to look to the sky and then tells you how to photograph various astronomical objects in the sky. Tips on how to select a pair of binoculars for beginning the study of astronomy are outlined. For advanced astronomers, tips on how to purchase and then use a telescope are provided.

Part Two, KEEP UP TO DATE, is a handy reference section that provides information on astronomy magazines, newsletters, calendars and notes. The top fifty magazine articles on astronomy, written in the past fifteen years, are listed for teachers to read along with the names of various teacher resource centers where you can obtain astronomy information. Also featured in this section are the names and addresses of astronomy organizations, book clubs, book companies, books, and companies that have catalogs, observation aids, star charts, computer software and other astronomy supplies and materials available. Once you and your students begin to look to the sky, you will want to do the activities in Part Three, HOW TO CONTINUE TO LOOK TO THE SKY. This chapter will give you many ideas for the development of instructional materials that you can actually make and use. Included in this chapter are over twenty-five handy instructional aids that you can make with minimal equipment. Also included are six pairs of seasonal sky transparency masters, handy fold-out charts for easy display, and thirty-five constellation copymasters. The latter can also be used to make transparencies. Hopefully, you and your students will find these to be very useful in your study of astronomy.

As you continue to grow in your knowledge of astronomy, it is hoped that you and your students will take the time to "look to the sky" as an integral part of each day in your lives.

PART ONE

HOW TO BEGIN TO LOOK TO THE SKY

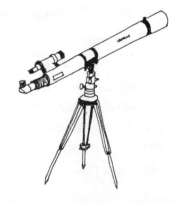

HOW TO PHOTOGRAPH THE NIGHT SKY

At some point during your study of astronomy, you will feel a need to bring the night sky into your classroom. The use of a local planetarium makes this easy and convenient. If you do not have a planetarium, however, a legitimate substitute is to use a camera. Much of what is beautiful and interesting in the sky to the unaided eye can be easily captured on film with ordinary equipment. About all that is needed is a camera with a shutter that can be locked open for time exposures, a cable release to reduce camera movement during the exposure and a stable tripod.

While there are many different types of cameras, only one is ideal for astrophotography—the 35mm single lens reflex (SLR). When you look through the viewfinder of this camera, you actually see what the film sees. Be sure your camera has a "B" or bulb setting. This will allow you to keep the shutter open for any length of time and thus expose the film longer. Film has the unique property of being able to collect and store light. Thus, the longer the exposure, the brighter the star images on the film. This also allows very dim stars, which are otherwise invisible to the eye, to become visible in the picture.

Since many of the pictures you want to take require a time exposure, it is necessary to hold the camera steady. This is accomplished by mounting the camera on a rigid tripod. This prevents the camera from moving and thus blurring the images on the film. The use of a cable release is optional. The cable release usually fits into the shutter button of the camera. The use of a cable release also helps to keep the picture sharp by minimizing camera vibrations when the shutter is opened and closed.

The final necessary consideration to take successful sky pictures is the film. The more sensitive a particular film is to light, the shorter the required exposure necessary to capture starlight. Shorter exposures will minimize the effects of the motion of the stars due to the earth's rotation. The film's sensitivity or film speed, given as an ISO number, is generally listed on the film box or on the instruction sheet provided with the film. The higher the ISO number, the faster the film. This means shorter exposure times for you and your photographs.

FROM STAR TRAILS TO CONSTELLATIONS

You can begin to take pictures of objects in the sky by photographing simple star trails. Photos of star trails are easy to make. They are further enhanced when combined with a unique landscape. Simply load your camera with ISO 200 film or any faster film. TIP: Color slide film is the best to use from a processing standpoint and it is the least expensive. Set the camera opening (f stop) to its widest setting, usually f/1.8 or f/2.0. Mount the camera on a tripod. Aim the camera at the sky and open the shutter. Because the stars do not remain stationary in the sky during the exposure, they will show up as streaks of light on the final picture. The longer the shutter is left open, the longer the trails appear on the film. As always, make a written record of each picture you take, noting its contents and "f" stop. This will come in handy later on in your study of astronomy.

Photographers who live in or near a large city should be aware of light pollution, a potential problem in taking successful pictures. Light from bright city lights is scattered and reflected by the atmosphere. This tends to fog your film, washing out star images and making long exposures (fifteen seconds or more) impractical. If possible, travel well away from city lights before taking astrophotographs. Your photographs will then have high contrast between star images and the sky.

To capture the stars of the night sky as pinpoints of light on film, simply reduce the length of exposure time. When using a normal lens with a 50mm focal length on your camera, exposures of stars near the *celestial poles* can be as long as twenty-five seconds and show no trails. At the *celestial equator*, exposures should be no longer than fifteen seconds to ensure pinpoint star images. Using lenses of shorter focal lengths will allow you to increase exposure time without the presence of star trails. With these shorter exposures, the patterns of constellations in the sky will stand out when the slide is projected on the screen.

Techniques used to photograph other celestial phenomena are similar to those used to photograph constellations. Exposure times will vary with light conditions, but the basics are the same. Lunar and planetary conjunctions are excellent subjects. The alignment of the moon with a bright star or planet along with an interesting foreground makes for an exciting and beautiful picture. And by all means, use your camera and acquired techniques to photograph that mysterious celestial traveler, the comet.

STAR TRAILS

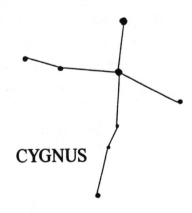

CYGNUS

FROM CONSTELLATIONS TO PLANETS

Project: Retrograde Motion of the Planets

The observation of planets against a background of stars is an interesting challenge. It may take you several months to determine various movements of the planets. The farther a planet is from the earth the slower its motion against a background of stars. The planet Mars, being fairly close to the earth, is a good example to observe as it is at times visible during most of the night and moves fast enough in its orbit to see it change position in the sky over a relatively short period of time.

Mars and the other superior planets (Jupiter, Saturn, Uranus, Neptune and Pluto) appear to move backwards (retrograde) at opposition (planet 180° opposite the sun; that is, when the sun sets the planet rises) as the earth passes them in their orbit. The inferior planets, Mercury and Venus, also move retrograde in a similar way as they pass the earth in its orbit.

Using available reference materials such as those found in *Sky and Telescope, Astronomy, The Observer's Handbook* and the *Sky Calendar*, determine when Mars will be at opposition. Then for three months before and after the opposition date, photograph the planet using the same techniques as you used for photographing the constellations. Do this at least once a week. Each photograph should be taken with the same camera, film, lens opening and exposure. Be sure that written records of each exposure are kept for later reference. For large group use, it is best to use color slide film. It is also possible to use black and white film if additional prints can be made from the negatives. At the end of six months you will have pictures that show the motion of Mars in the night sky.

To use the slides, tape a large sheet of paper to the classroom wall. Project the first slide onto the paper and mark the position of the fixed stars along with the position of the planet. Remember to mark the date on which the picture was taken next to the position of the planet. Project the next slide of the set onto the paper. Orient the paper so that the reference stars overlap the ones drawn previously on the paper. Again, mark the position of Mars. Continue this process until the entire set of slides is projected and sketched on the paper. Remove the paper from the wall. Have students connect the dots that represent the various locations of Mars. Make sure that this is done in order from the first picture to the last. Then have your students answer the questions on page 5.

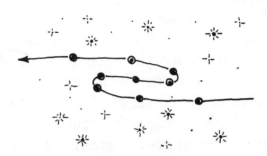

RETROGRADE MOTION OF MARS

Questions to Answer

1. What is the shape of the path of Mars in the sky? _____

2. On what day did retrograde motion begin? _____

3. Does the brightness of Mars change during the six-month period? _____ If so, at what time was Mars at its brightest?_____

METEOR PHOTOGRAPHY

A further challenge to capture celestial events on film lies in meteor photography. What makes this type of celestial show difficult is the unpredictable nature of the meteor, or what is popularly called a "shooting star." A streak of light that lasts only a few seconds in any part of the sky is truly a challenge. Your chances of capturing a meteor on film will be enhanced during one of the many meteor showers when the *radiant* (the point in the sky from which the meteor appears to come) is high overhead. A list of meteor showers is found below.

Use the same photographic techniques that you mastered to produce star trails. Aim your camera slightly away from the radiant of the meteor shower. Open the shutter of your camera. Sit back and wait. If after several minutes a meteor has not crossed through the field of view of your camera, stop the exposure and start again. The length of exposure depends on how bright the sky is because of nearby lights. As soon as you suspect that a meteor was seen by the camera, stop the exposure, advance the film, aim the camera in a different part of the sky and try again. The camera does all the work for you so just lie back and enjoy the celestial fireworks.

Important Monthly Meteor Showers

Meteor Shower Name	Begins	Maximum	Ends	Location and Position of Radiant
Quandrantids	1/1	1/3	January 6	Northern Bootes
Lyrids	4/9	4/22	April 24	Hercules
Eta Aquarids	5/2	5/4	May 7	Aquarius
Delta Aquarids	7/15	7/28	August 15	Aquarius
Perseids	7/25	8/12*	August 18	Cassiopeia
Orionids	10/16	10/21	October 26	Northern Orion
Leonids	11/15	11/17*	November 19	Leo
Geminids	12/7	12/14*	December 15	Gemini
Ursids	12/17	12/22	December 24	Ursa Minor

*Be sure to see these; they are brilliant.

METEOR SHOWER

METEOR CRATER, ARIZONA

NAKED EYE ASTRONOMY TO BINOCULARS

"I sure would like to learn more about astronomy and the night sky, but I really cannot do it without a telescope to help me." This statement is often made by young astronomy enthusiasts, and yet nothing can be further from the truth. All beginning astronomers have what it takes to discover the wonders of the heavens just as Copernicus, Kepler, Tycho and Galileo did—their eyes! By far the best way to start out in observational astronomy is with a good star chart (a revolving star chart that shows the constellation outlines for an entire year or a monthly star chart found in astronomy magazines are excellent choices) and the naked eye. Binoculars or a simple telescope can be added later once a strong background and a true interest in observing the night sky has been demonstrated.

There are many reasons why one should start an observational program with just the unaided eye. It is easy, inexpensive and involves no complicated equipment to frustrate the novice. It can be done anywhere and anytime the skies are clear as well as by everyone. Familiarity with the night sky is essential for putting a good pair of binoculars or a telescope to their maximum use.

You will want to take the first step of mastering the heavens by learning what constellations are visible at various times of the year and which ones will be visible during the course of a single evening. From an observational site away from city lights (if possible), make yourself comfortable by either lying on a blanket on the ground or in a lawn chair. Allow your eyes to become adapted to the darkness. This will usually take from fifteen minutes to just over one-half hour. If you need a flashlight to check your star charts, place a piece of red cellophane over the lens to prevent light blindness. A single layer of a paper bag also works well as a substitute for cellophane. Remember, do not try to do too much your first time out. You want to minimize confusion while learning what the sky has to offer. Start your study by identifying the constellations and their bright stars by name. Bright stars and constellations serve as maps for later observation with binoculars or a telescope. They will help you locate nebulae, galaxies, star clusters and other objects that you are unable to see with your naked eye.

There are many other activities for you to do to further your knowledge of what is in the sky. For instance, notice the motion of the stars during the evening (this motion is due to the west to east rotation of the earth). Some will rise in the east, march high across the sky and set in the west while others seem to circle about the North Star, Polaris, without ever rising or setting. You might want to see how far they move in an hour.

If the moon happens to be visible anytime during the night, watch its eastward motion against the background stars as it moves in its orbit (the moon's westward motion is due to the rotation of the earth). A keen observer will notice the motion in an hour or so.

Once you are comfortable finding your way around the sky, you are ready to try hunting down individual celestial objects such as double stars, star clusters, nebulae and galaxies. This is where some sort of optical aid is necessary. For the serious beginner, a telescope still may not be the ideal instrument. A good pair of binoculars will go a long way in serving this need.

FROM BINOCULARS TO ...

Inexpensive, easy to handle and capable of providing some truly memorable views of the night sky, binoculars are an ideal instrument for the beginning observer. Astronomy with binoculars can be done at a picnic table, from a hammock, from really anywhere. There is no need to take the time to set up and align a telescope, something that might discourage the beginner. Simply lift the binoculars toward the sky and enjoy the view.

Although less complicated than a good telescope, there are several important points about binoculars that must be made. A pair of binoculars is described by their magnification and lens diameter. For example, 7″ x 35″ binoculars will magnify distant objects seven times and will have light-gathering (objective) lenses 35 millimeters in diameter. Greater magnification will yield a larger image but the unsteadiness of hand-held binoculars will increase. The diameter of the objective lens determines the ability of the binoculars to detect faint objects. One other point of importance in selecting a quality pair of binoculars is the *field of view*. The field of view is generally given as being some number of feet at a thousand yards distance. Fifty feet at a thousand yards is equivalent to just about one degree, so to convert to a degree measurement (which is what distances between stars in the sky are measured in), simply divide by 50. For example, a field of "500 feet at a thousand yards" corresponds to about 500 ÷ 50 or ten degrees.

With a good pair of 10 x 50 binoculars, many star clusters, nebulae and galaxies will easily pop into view if you know where to look. To know where to look, a more detailed star chart than the one used to identify the constellations is necessary. There are several sky charts available from any of the publishing companies listed on pages 20 and 21.

If the beginning astronomer's interest continues, it will not be long before binoculars will give way to a first telescope. The selection of a telescope is much more involved and should be done very carefully.

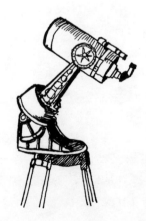

TELESCOPES

The time will come when the beginning astronomer earns the right to have his/ her first telescope. Many hours of studying and observing the sky with the naked eye and a pair of binoculars can only be rewarded with a telescope. The selection of a first telescope is a much more involved process than selecting and buying a pair of binoculars. There are many more considerations, for example, type, size, mount and, of course, cost. We will begin to understand the selection of a telescope by first exploring the types available.

The job of any telescope is to collect light from distant sources and focus it into an image which is then looked at with an eyepiece. The optical designs of telescopes are many and quite varied, but most of them available to the amateur astronomer fit into one of the three major categories—refractor, reflector and catadioptrics or compound telescopes.

The refracting 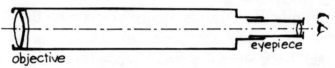 telescope is the type familiar to most everyone— the long tube with a glass lens at one end and eyepiece at the other end, all mounted on a tall tripod. The earliest telescopes made in the early seventeenth century were simple refractors. The objective lens of the refractor gathers the faint light from distant stars, bends the light and brings it to a focal point at the eyepiece. The eyepiece is then used to enlarge the image that is formed by the objective lens. A major problem with refractors is color distortion. If you have ever played with a prism, you know that white light can be broken into many colors called the spectrum. A refracting telescope acts somewhat like a prism as it bends light, so star images may have odd colors around the edges. If equipped with an achromatic lens to prevent color fringing and a sturdy mount, a small refractor can provide outstanding views of the moon, planets and star clusters. In most cases a good 2.4″ (60mm) refractor is an excellent choice for a first telescope. Refractors do, however, have one drawback that cannot be corrected . . . COST. When observing nebulae, galaxies and star clusters where light gathering counts, refractors cost much more than any other common type of telescope with the same aperture.

The reflector, popularly called a Newto- nian reflec- tor because the first one was built by Sir Isaac Newton, is quite simple in design. A highly polished parabolic glass disk coated usually with aluminum or silver at the bottom of a long open tube serves as the objective. Light enters the tube and travels to the objective mirror where it is reflected back to the open end. At that point a small secondary mirror, supported by three or four small vanes reflects the light out of the tube to the eyepiece. Reflectors with a 4"-6" mirror and a good equatorial mount, although costing more than a 2.4" refractor (reflectors actually provide the largest aperture for the lowest cost) is an excellent choice for the most serious first-time observer. However, one must be careful when selecting a reflector bought in a toy or department store. If the objective mirror is spherical instead of parabolic, the images formed by the mirror will be in focus at the center of the field of view and become progressively out of focus near the edges. Be sure that the mirror in your telescope is parabolic.

Catadioptrics or compound telescopes combine the best features of both refractors and reflectors resulting in a compact lightweight instrument that is very portable and easy to set up. The folding of the light path by a series of reflections yields a telescope 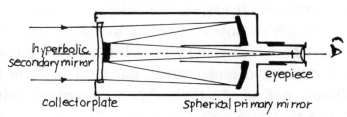 much smaller in size than both refractors and reflectors with the same aperture.

Incoming light enters a sealed tube through a thin correcting lens, strikes the objective mirror and is reflected back up to a small secondary mirror on the back of the correcting lens. The secondary mirror reflects the light back down through a hole in the objective and out to the eyepiece. All compound telescopes are made with lenses corrected for color fringing and a parabolic mirror. The compound telescope sounds like it is the best of both worlds, but it does have one major drawback, COST. An 8" catadioptric can cost up to 75 percent more than a comparably equipped 8" Newtonian reflector and just slightly more than a 4" refractor. The catadioptric is *not* a good choice for a young observer's first telescope. It does make an excellent telescope as one goes away from a small refractor or reflector.

Whether you decide to buy a refractor, reflector or catadioptric telescope, more than anything else, the diameter and quality of the telescope's objective lens or mirror determines how a telescope will perform and what you will be able to see with it. A refracting lens not correcting for color fringing or a spherical mirror in a reflector will quickly discourage any observer from using the telescope again.

The second most important thing to look for in a telescope is a well-built, steady mount. There is nothing worse than trying to find a faint nebulae with a telescope that just will not hold steady. Stay away from telescopes mounted on long, thin metal legs held together with a few tiny screws. It is a good idea to try out the telescope first in a store if you can. You should be able to touch the tube, focus and change eyepieces without any resulting wobble.

Most telescopes for beginners come equipped with either an *alt-azimuth* or simple *equatorial* mount. The alt-azimuth mount will usually be found on small refractors. *Alt* stands for altitude and *azimuth* refers to horizontal movement. In other words, the telescope has two basic motions, up and down and left and right. The main advantage of an alt-azimuth mount is its simplicity. The main disadvantage is that the left to right motion of the telescope is not the same as the movement of the stars in the sky. You may have some trouble at first with objects drifting out of the field of view during extended observing sessions, but with a little time and practice the problem will soon be eliminated.

An equatorial mount is usually found on most reflectors and all catadioptric telescopes. The mount is designed such that one of the two axes of motion always points to the North Star. The entire telescope can then be rotated around this axis from side to side (east to west). The east to west movement follows the motion of the sky, so once you find an object you can keep it in the field of view with just a few minor adjustments. As with the alt-azimuth mount, the equatorial mount also has an up and down motion. If the mount is properly aligned with the North Star, you will not need to use the up and down motion to keep a star centered in the telescope.

The first question most beginners ask about any telescope is "How much power can I get?" Advertising claims for high magnifications of 300x to 500x are very misleading and usually mean BE CAREFUL! There is a practical limit of magnification with all optical instruments. For telescopes, that limit is about 50x-60x per inch of aperture. For a 2.4″ refractor it means the useful high power range lies between 120x and 144x. Magnification given by a telescope depends upon the *focal length* of both the objective lens or mirror and the eyepiece being used. The focal length is the distance from a lens or a curved mirror to the point where an image is formed and is usually expressed in units of millimeters. To determine the magnification that is being used, divide the focal length of the telescope by the focal length of the eyepiece. For example, a 900mm telescope with an eyepiece of 20mm will provide a magnification of 45x. Theoretically, there is no limit to the magnifying power of an instrument. As we use eyepieces of smaller and smaller focal lengths, thus giving higher power, the image becomes more and more fuzzy, though larger. Finally, the fuzziness becomes so extreme that objects are seen less clearly than those at a lower power. So beware of ads that claim to sell "400x DELUXE 60mm refractor. Your best buy!"

One final bit of information concerning telescope selection, and one that is usually overlooked and misunderstood, is the focal ratio of the telescope (abbreviated *f/ratio*). What does it mean to say a telescope has an f/ratio of f/5.6 or f/10 and what does this number have to do with the overall performance of the telescope? The number is simply the focal length of the telescope divided by the diameter of the objective. For example, an 8-inch (200mm) catadioptric telescope with a focal length of 78 inches (2000mm) has an f/ratio of f/10. Telescopes with low f/ratios are considered "fast" and will produce a brighter image when compared to an identically sized telescope with a high f/ratio. Telescopes with high f/ratios are considered "slow." Lower f/ratios on any given sized telescope will lower the magnification for a given eyepiece, and it will also produce a wider field of view.

Once you have read about telescopes and have decided to buy your first one, remember to keep it simple. Select a telescope that is light enough, yet sturdy, so you can carry it easily and set it up by yourself. Keep it small so that you can easily move it to areas where skies are darker or so that you can take it on vacation. Avoid telescopes with a lot of gadgets or accessories attached to them. These are usually put there so that you think you are getting a good deal when in fact you will probably never use or need them. A telescope is a major investment in time and money. That is why it is important for you to think carefully about what is best for you.

With their first telescope set up in the backyard, many people are disappointed with their initial views. "What?" "That's the famous Orion Nebulae?" "Where are the beautiful colors and long thin wisps of gas?" "Why is it so small?" "How come it doesn't look like the pictures?" Most objects in the sky will never look like the photographs that you have marveled at in astronomy books and magazines. Many of those photos were taken by using some of the world's largest telescopes, special films and extra long exposures. Do not expect your new 6″ reflector to provide the same view that the 200″ Hale telescope on Mt. Palomar provides.

As with any piece of equipment, a telescope is only as good as the person who uses it. Who knows, maybe with hard work and a lot of studying, you will be able to someday use the 200″ on Mt. Palomar.

PART TWO

KEEP UP TO DATE

READ THE TOP FIFTY "HOW TO" ASTRONOMY
ARTICLES PUBLISHED IN THE PAST FIFTEEN YEARS

Subject Area: Astrophotography

Title of Article	Magazine	Month and Year of Publication
"How to Get Started in Astrophotography"	Astronomy	April 1987
"Astrophotography Without a Telescope"	Astronomy	January 1987
"How to Process Color Astro Slides"	Astronomy	September 1986
"Camera Lenses for Deep Sky Photography"	Astronomy	August 1986
"Fundamentals of Astrophotography"	Astronomy	March 1986
"How to Get Started in Piggyback Astrophotography"	Astronomy	November 1985
"Celestial Photography Is Easier Than You Think"	Astronomy	October 1985
"Gentle Art of Comet Photography"	Astronomy	August 1985
"Photographing Meteors in Winter"	Astronomy	November 1984
"Add Drama and Interest to Your Astrophotos"	Astronomy	January 1984
"How Much Sky Can My Camera Capture"	Astronomy	June 1982
"Bare Bones Astrophotography"	Astronomy	March 1981
"Wide Field Sky Photography"	Astronomy	January 1980
"This Is Astrophotography" (Shows what the amateur can do)	Astronomy	September 1979
"How to Photograph a Spaceship" (Satellites)	Astronomy	June 1979
"Exposure in Astrophotography"	Astronomy	July 1978
"Astrophotography with Camera Only"	Astronomy	June 1978
"Astrophotography with Telephoto Lenses"	Astronomy	July 1977
"Is Faster Better?" (Color slide film evaluation)	Astronomy	December 1976
"Astrophotography in Spite of Myself"	Astronomy	April 1976
"Photograph a Comet" (Camera and tripod)	Astronomy	February 1976
"Astrophotography: A Woman's View"	Astronomy	February 1976
"Astrophotographic Routes" (All camera combinations explained)	Astronomy	May 1975
"The Night Tourists"	Astronomy	February 1975
"Piggyback Astrophotography"	Astronomy	January 1975
"Sky Photography Without a Telescope"	Astronomy	November 1974
"Catch a Falling Star"	Astronomy	August 1974
"It's Simple to Photograph Constellations"	Astronomy	November 1973
"An Evaluation of Films for Astrophotography"	Sky and Telescope	May 1980
"Starlight and Patience"	Sky and Telescope	April 1980
"Astrophotography: Planning Pays Off"	Sky and Telescope	February 1979
"On the Road to Better Astrophotos I"	Sky and Telescope	June 1977
"On the Road to Better Astrophotos II"	Sky and Telescope	May 1977
"On the Road to Better Astrophotos III"	Sky and Telescope	June 1977
"Hints on Photographing the Solar Eclipse"	Sky and Telescope	June 1972

Subject Area: Constellations

"The Stars of Autumn"	Astronomy	September 1984
"Find the Summer Constellations"	Astronomy	June 1984
"Probing the Constellations of Spring"	Astronomy	March 1984
"Learn the Winter Constellations"	Astronomy	December 1983
"Learning the Constellations"—Part IV	Astronomy	October 1978
"Naked Eye Astronomy"—Part II	Astronomy	August 1978
"Learning the Constellations"—Part III	Astronomy	July 1978
"Naked Eye Astronomy"—Part I	Astronomy	June 1978
"Learning the Constellations"—Part II	Astronomy	April 1978
"Learning the Constellations"—Part I	Astronomy	December 1977

Subject Area: Astronomy Equipment

"Binoculars for Astronomy"	Astronomy	December 1986
"1986 Astronomy Guide to Telescopes"	Astronomy	October 1986
"Discovering Binocular Astronomy"	Astronomy	December 1985
"How to Buy a Telescope for a Child"	Astronomy	October 1980
"Binoculars for Star Gazing"	Astronomy	March 1977

READ ASTRONOMY BOOKS WISELY AND REGULARLY

Miller, R., & W. Hartmann. *The Grand Tour: A Traveler's Guide to the Solar System.* New York: Workman Publishers, 1981. (Art)

Covington, M. *Astrophotography for the Amateur.* New York: Cambridge Press, 1985. (Astrophotography)

Sherrod, P. *A Complete Manual of Amateur Astronomy.* Englewood Cliffs, N.J.: Prentice-Hall, 1981. (Amateur Astronomy)

Muirden, J. *Astronomy with Binoculars.* New York: Arco Publishers, 1984. (Binoculars)

Whitney, C. *Whitney's Star Finder.* New York: Knopf Publishers, 1985. (Children's Book)

Sagan, C., & A. Druyan. *Comet.* New York: Random House, 1985. (Comets)

McDonough, T. *The Search for Extraterrestrial Intelligence: Listening for Life in the Cosmos.* New York: Wiley, 1987. (Extraterrestrial Life)

Kaufmann, W. *Galaxies and Quasars.* San Francisco: W.H. Freeman, 1979. (Galaxies and Quasars)

Critchton, M. *The Andromeda Strain.* New York: Dell Publishers, 1969. (General Fiction)

Menzel, D., & J. Pasachoff. *A Field Guide to the Stars and Planets.* Boston: Houghton-Mifflin, 1983. (Manual)

Schaaf, F. *Wonders of the Sky.* New York: Dover Publications, 1983. (Manual)

Sagan, C. et al. *Murmurs of the Earth: The Voyager Interstellar Record.* New York: Random House, 1978. (Music)

Krupp, E. *Echoes of the Ancient Skies: The Astronomy of Lost Civilizations.* New York: Harper & Row, 1983. (Nontechnical Astronomy)

Updike, J. *Facing Nature.* New York: Knopf Publishers, 1985. (Poetry)

Abell, G., & B. Singer. *Science and the Paranormal.* New York: Scribners, 1981. (Psychology)

Burnham, R. *Burnham's Celestial Handbook.* New York: Dover Publications, 1978. (Reference Book)

Fraknoi, A. *Universe in the Classroom.* San Francisco: W.H. Freeman, 1985. (Science Fiction)

Frazier, K. *Solar System.* Alexandria: Time-Life Books, 1985. (Solar System)

Clark, D. *Superstars.* New York: McGraw-Hill, 1984. (Stars)

Noyes, R. *The Sun, Our Star.* Cambridge, Mass.: Harvard University Press, 1982. (Sun)

Field, G., & E. Chaisson. *The Invisible Universe: Probing the Frontiers of Astrophysics.* Boston: Birkhauser, 1985. (Technical Astronomy)

Tucker, W., & K. Tucker. *The Cosmic Inquiries: Modern Telescopes and Their Makers.* Cambridge, Mass.: Harvard University Press, 1986. (Telescopes)

Jastrow, R. *Red Giants and White Dwarfs.* New York: Norton, 1979. (Universe)

Trefil, J. *Space Time and Infinity.* New York: Pantheon Books, 1985. (Universe)

READ ASTRONOMY MAGAZINES REGULARLY

Sky and Telescope
Sky Publishing Corporation
49 Bay State Road
Cambridge, MA 02238

Astronomy
Astromedia Corporation
1027 N. 7th Street
Milwaukee, WI 53233

Odyssey
Astromedia Corporation
1027 N. 7th Street
Milwaukee, WI 53233

The Astrograph
P.O. Box 2283
Arlington, VA 22202

Space World
Amherst, WI 54406

Journal of the ALPO
Association of Lunar and Planetary
  Observers
P.O. Box 16131
San Francisco, CA 94116

Comet News Service
P.O. Box TDR, No. 92
Truckee, CA 95734

Meteor News
c/o Wanda Simmons
Rt. 3, Box 424-99
Calahan, FL 32011

Star Date
The Astronomy News Report
RLM 15.308
The University of Texas at Austin
Austin, TX 78712

WRITE FOR ASTRONOMY NEWSLETTERS, CALENDARS AND NOTES

News from the Naval Observatory
34th and Massachusetts Ave., N.W.
Washington, D.C. 20390
(Send for free monthly newsletter.
Make request on school stationery.)

Sky Calendar
Abrams Planetarium
Michigan State Universtiy
East Lansing, MI 48824
(Monthly sky calendar and evening
skies)

The Department of Physics
Furman University
Greenville, SC 29613
(Astronomy information)

WRITE TO THE NATIONAL AERONAUTICS AND SPACE (NASA) TEACHER RESOURCE CENTERS

Ames Research Center
Teacher Resource Center
Mail Stop 204-7
Moffet Field, CA 94035
(415) 694-6077

Goddard Space Flight Center
Teacher Resource Center
Mail Code 130.3
Greenbelt, MD 20771
(301) 344-8981

Jet Propulsion Laboratory
Science & Mathematics Teaching
Resource Center
c/o Education Outreach-MSTRC
Mail Stop 520
Pasadena, CA 91109
(818) 354-4321

Johnson Space Center
Teacher Resource Center AP 4
Houston, TX 77058
(713) 783-3455

Kennedy Space Center
Educator Resource Library
Mail Code ERL
Kennedy Space Center, FL 32899
(305) 867-4090

Langley Research Center
Teacher Resource Center
Mail Stop 146
Hampton, VA 23665
(804) 865-4468

Lewis Research Center
Teacher Resource Center
Mail Stop 8-1
Cleveland, OH 44135
(216) 267-1187

Marshall Space Flight Center
Teacher Resource Center
Space and Rocket Center
Tranquility Base
Huntsville, AL 35812
(205) 837-3400 Ext. 36

National Space Technology Lab
Teacher Resource Center
Building 1200
NSTL Station, MS 39529
(601) 688-3338

WRITE FOR ASTRONOMY TEACHING RESOURCES

MMI Space Science Corporation
Dept. ST-85
2950 Wymann Parkway
Box 19907
Baltimore, MD 21211

1985 Astronomy Resource Guide
West Virginia University Bookstore
College Avenue
Morgantown, WV 26506

The Night Sky Company
1334 Brommer Street
Santa Cruz, CA 95062

READ ABOUT AND USE INTERDISCIPLINARY ASTRONOMY MATERIALS

(A = Art) (F = Fiction) (L = Law) (M = Music) (P = Poetry) (PS = Psychology)

(A)
Chaikin, A. "Images of Other Worlds," *Sky and Telescope*, November, 1982.

(A)
Gardner, M. "The Eerie Mathematical Art of Maurits Escher," *Scientific American*, April, 1966.

(A)
Natabartold, A. "Some Problems for Art Objects in Extra-Terrestrial Space," *Leonardo*, Spring, 1975.

(A)
Olson, R. "Giotto's Portrait of Halley's Comet," *Scientific American*, May, 1979.

(A)
Pander, H. "An Artist's Astronomical Odyssey," *Sky and Telescope*, January, 1979.

(A)
Reis. R., & A. Braun. "Beyond Our Time: An Interview with Chesley Bonestell," *Mercury*, May-June, 1977.

(A)
Turner, R. "Extraterrestrial Landscapes Through the Eyes of a Sculptor," *Leonardo*, Winter, 1972.

(F)
Friedman, A. "Contemporary American Physics Fiction," *American Journal of Physics*, May, 1979.

(F)
Gingerich, O. "Great Conjunctions Tycho, and Shakespeare," *Sky and Telescope*, May, 1981.

(L)
Christol, C. "Space Law: Justice for the New Frontier," *Sky and Telescope*, November, 1984.

(L)
Freitas, R. "Metalaw and Interstellar Relations," *Mercury*, March-April, 1977.

(L)
Hansen, J. "The Crime of Galileo," *Science 81*, March, 1981.

(L)
Katz, C. "The Prosecution Never Rests: The Trials of Galileo Galilei," *The California State Bar Journal*, March-April, 1977.

(M)
Fraknoi, A. "The Music of the Spheres: Astronomical Sources of Musical Inspiration," *Mercury*, May-June, 1977.

(M)
Fraknoi, A. "More Music of the Spheres," *Mercury*, November-December, 1979.

(M)
Rodgers, J., & W. Ruff. "Kepler's Harmony of the World: A Realization for the Ear," *American Scientist*, May-June, 1979.

(M)
Ronan, C. "Astronomy and Music," *Sky and Telescope*, September, 1975.

(M)
Ronan, C. "William Herschel and His Music," *Sky and Telescope*, March, 1981.

(P)
Ackerman, D. "The Poetry of Diane Ackerman," *Mercury*, July-August, 1978.

(P)
Byard, M. "Poetic Response to the Copernican Revolution," *Scientific American*, June, 1977.

(P)
Carter, T. "Geoffrey Chaucer: Amateur Astronomer?" *Sky and Telescope*, March, 1982.

(P)
Fraknoi, A., & A. Friedman. "Images of the Universe," *Mercury*, March-April, 1975.

(PS)
Restle, F. "The Moon Illusion Explained on the Basis of Relative Size," *Science*, February 20, 1970.

(PS)
Saunders, F. "The Moon Illusion," *Mercury*, March-April, 1976.

WRITE FOR INFORMATION

Write for information on astronomy organizations (O), book clubs and book companies (BC), instruments (I), observational aids (OA), star charts (SC), computer software (CS) and miscellaneous supplies and equipment (MS).

(O) Astronomical Society of the Pacific 1290 24th Avenue San Francisco, CA 94122	**(BC)** Astronomy Book Club Riverside, NJ 08075-9889	**(BC)** The Observer's Guide P.O. Box 35 Natrona Heights, PA 15065
(BC) Willman-Bell, Inc. P.O. Box 35025 Richmond, VA 23235	**(I)** AD-LIBS Astronomics 2401 Tee Circle Norman, OK 73069	**(I)** Bausch and Lomb Astronomical Division 135 Prestige Park Circle East Hartford, CT 06108
(I) Celestron International P.O. Box 3578 2835 Columbia Street Torrance, CA 90503	**(I)** Edmund Scientific 101 East Gloucester Pike Barrington, NJ 08007	**(I)** Lumicon 2111 Research Drive Suites 4-5 Livermore, CA 94550
(I) Mack Optical & Machine-Tool P.O. Box 541-T Scranton, PA 18501	**(I)** Meade Instruments Corporation 1675 Toronto Way Costa Mesa, CA 92626	**(I)** Orion Telescope Center 421 Soquel Avenue P.O. 1158 Santa Cruz, CA 95062
(I) Parks Optical 270 East Street Simi Valley, CA 93065	**(I)** Roger W. Tuthill, Inc. 11 Tanglewood Lane Mountainside, NJ 07092	**(I)** Telescope Exchange 4347 Sepulveda Blvd. Culver City, CA 90203
(I) Unitron Instruments 175 Express Street Plainview, NY 11803	**(I)** University Optics P.O. Box 1025 Ann Arbor, MI 48106	**(OA)** Astro Cards P.O. Box 35 Natrona Heights, PA 15065
(OA) Astro Tech 101 W. Main P.O. Box 2001 Ardmore, OK 73402	**(OA)** Everything in the Universe 5248 Lawton Avenue Oakland, CA 94618	**(OA)** Peninsula Scientific 2185 Park Blvd. Palo Alto, CA 94306
(SC) Edmund Mag 5 Star Atlas Edmund Scientific 101 E. Glouscester Pike Barrington, NJ 08007	**(SC)** Sky Atlas 2000.0 Sky Publishing Corporation 49 Bay State Road Cambridge, MA 02238	**(CS)** American Only, Inc. Science and Technology Software Division 13361 Frati Lane Sebastopol, CA 95472

(CS)	(CS)	(CS)
Andromeda Software, Inc. P.O. Box 1361 Williamsville, NY 14221	Astronomical Society of the Pacific 1290 24th Avenue San Francisco, CA 94122	COMPress P.O. Box 102 Wentworth, NH 03282

(CS)	(CS)	(CS)
E & M Software Company 95 Richardson Road North Cheimsford, MA 01863	Earl Enterprises 440 Harrel Drive Spartanburg, SC 29302	Imaginova, Inc. P.O. Box 4469 Warren, NJ 07060

(CS)	(CS)	(CS)
Light Software 1850 Union Street #252 San Francisco, CA 94123	Lightspeed Software 2124 Kittredge Street Suite 185 Berkeley, CA 94704	Tachyon Systems Astroware Products 55 Hillside Road Sparta, NJ 07871

(CS)	(CS)	(MS)
Visionary Software P.O. Box 1063 Midland, MI 48641-1063	Zephyr Services 306 South Homewood Avenue Pittsburgh, PA 15208	Astromurals P.O. Box 7563 Washington, D.C. 20044 (Astronomical prints)

(MS)	(MS)	(MS)
Astro Works 175 Piedra Loop White Rock, NM 87544	Chest Works P.O. Box 26751 Wauwatosa, WI 53226 (T-shirts)	Cotton Express 832 W. Junior Terrace Chicago, IL 60613

(MS)	(MS)	(MS)
Farquahar Globes 5007 Warrington Avenue Philadelphia, PA 19143 (Celestial globes)	Hansen Planetarium Publications 1098 South 200 West Salt Lake City, UT 84101 (Slides, posters)	Optica b/c Company Sales/Service Division 4100 MacArthur Blvd. Oakland, CA 94619

(MS)	(MS)	(MS)
Robert T. Little P.O. Box E Brooklyn, NY 11202 (Astrophotography equipment)	Star Shirts P.O. Box 912 Mt. Shasta, CA 96067 (Shirts and sweatshirts)	Sundials, Inc. Sawyer Passway Fitchburg, MA 01420 (Sundials)

(MS)		
Wessex Design Group Box 542-A Farmington, NY 11735 (T-shirts)	YOUR CHOICE	YOUR CHOICE

STARGAZING NOTES

OBSERVER'S NAME _____ TIME _____

OBSERVING LOCATION _____ DATE _____

METHOD OF OBSERVATION

NAKED EYE _____   BINOCULARS _____   TELESCOPE _____
(SIZE)   (SIZE)

CELESTIAL OBJECTS OBSERVED: _____
_____
_____
_____
_____

VISUAL IMPRESSIONS: _____
_____
_____
_____
_____
_____
_____
_____

TELESCOPE/BINOCULAR VIEW

OBJECT_____

EYEPIECE _____   ADDITIONAL NOTES AND SKETCHES

MAGNIFICATION _____

Use the reverse side of this observing page to record any naked eye observations.

PART THREE

HOW TO CONTINUE TO LOOK TO THE SKY: INSTRUCTIONAL MATERIALS YOU CAN MAKE AND USE

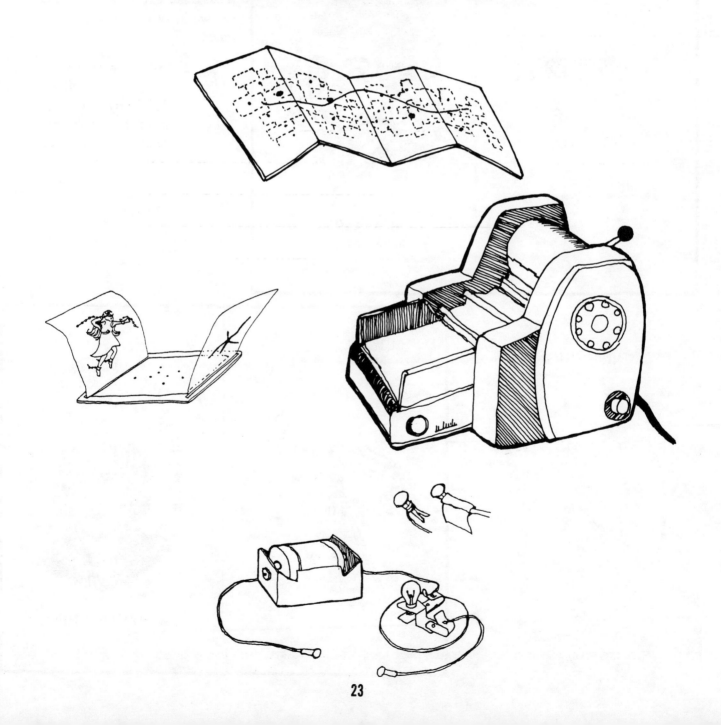

ADOPT AN ASTRONOMER

Begin your study of astronomy by having your students adopt an astronomer. These pages feature four mini booklets of famous astronomers. Have your students adopt one of the four astronomers or collect and make sketches of their favorite astronomer. Make a copy of each booklet for your students. (Consider making one set for the class or develop a class scrapbook of scientists.) Cut out each booklet. Fold on dotted line with the name and picture of the astronomer faceup on the right half of the cover. The matching symbol of the astronomer's contribution appears on the left half of the cover, which becomes the back cover of the booklet. Open the booklets. Have students print their names and pertinent information about the astronomers inside the booklets. Add additional pages as needed. Then encourage students to conduct a science fair experiment based on the works of the famous astronomer.

 TIP: See *Scientists Around the World* (1987) by Jerry De-Bruin for other portraits of scientists and related information.

BENJAMIN
BANNEKER

MARIA MITCHELL

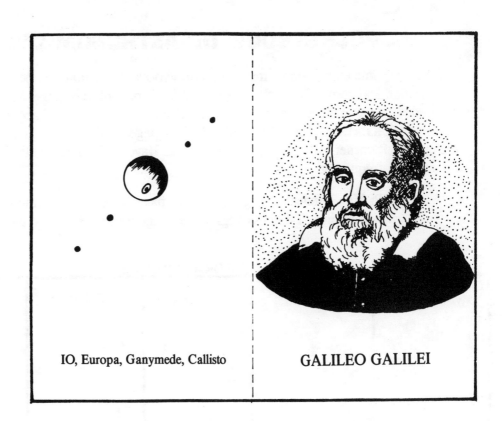

IO, Europa, Ganymede, Callisto

GALILEO GALILEI

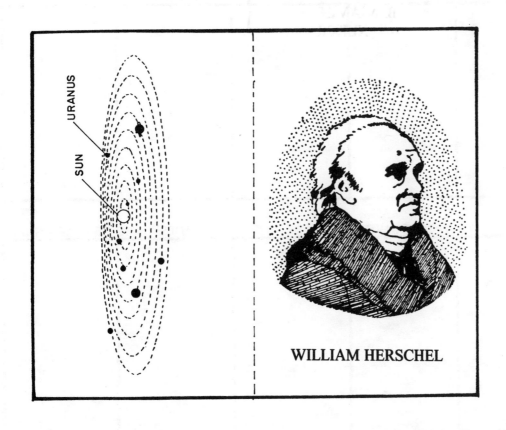

URANUS

SUN

WILLIAM HERSCHEL

POCKETBOOK OF ASTRONOMICAL TERMS

Here are some extra sample mini pages on various topics that can be added to a mini pocketbook of astronomical terms for each student. Make copies of this page and the following four pages as needed. Have students cut out and complete each mini page. Place mini pages of astronomical terms in alphabetical order. Add other topical pages. Clip, fasten or staple the pages together in the upper left corner. Add other pages as needed. Have students design their pocketbook of astronomy information frequently.

 TIP: Have students design their own pages using various media such as puzzles, bumper sticker sayings, T-shirt sayings and postage stamps related to the topic.

COVER PAGE   INFORMATION PAGE   BLANK PAGES FOR MORE TERMS

My Address	My Name	My Telephone #	My School		

BIBLIOGRAPHY PAGE   NOTE PAGE   SCRIBBLE PAGE

BUMPER STICKER PAGE   T-SHIRT SAYING PAGE   BLANK PAGES: TOPIC OF YOUR CHOICE

POCKETBOOK OF ASTRONOMICAL TERMS

ASTEROID:	NOTES:	ASTRONOMICAL UNIT:	NOTES:	ASTROPHYSICS:	NOTES:
Any of the thousands of small rocky objects that orbit around the sun, most of them between the orbits of Mars and Jupiter.	Largest asteroid is CERES whose width is about that of the state of Texas.	A unit of distance equal to the average distance between the earth and the sun. The abbreviation for astronomical unit is AU. One AU equals about 150 million kilometers (93 million miles).	It takes light eight minutes to travel one AU when it travels from the sun to the earth.	A branch of astronomy in which one studies the physical processes that regulate activity in the universe.	One would study astrophysics if one wanted to find out what causes a star to become bright.

BIG BANG:	NOTES:	BINARY STAR:	NOTES:	BLACK HOLE:	NOTES:
A big explosion long ago which most astronomers think gave rise to the universe. The "big bang" features clusters of galaxies moving apart from each other.	Some astronomers think that the "big bang" happened 15-20 billion years ago.	A system of two or more stars which orbit around each other.	The nearest star to our solar system is Alpha Centauri which has three stars, two like our sun and one dim red one. These all orbit around each other.	An object in the sky whose pull of gravity is so strong that nothing, even light, is able to escape from it.	Black holes are thought to be made when massive stars collapse at the ends of their lives.

COMET:	NOTES:	CONSTELLATION:	NOTES:	COSMOLOGY:	NOTES:
A small chunk of ice, dust and rocky material like a dirty snowball. Comets develop a tail when they get close to the sun.	A comet's tail is made up of gas and dust which has been driven off the surface of the comet by the sun's energy. Thus the comet's tail always points away from the sun.	A pattern of stars in the sky, named for an animal, person or object usually from mythology.	Astronomers have divided the sky into eighty-eight parts. Each part is named after a constellation located in that part.	A branch of astronomy in which one studies the origin, structure and evolution of the universe.	Most astronomers believe that the universe began with a "big bang" explosion long ago. Clusters of galaxies are moving away from each other as the result of the "big bang."

ECLIPSE:	NOTES:	EQUINOX:	NOTES:	GALAXY:	NOTES:
The blocking out of all or part of the light coming from one object by another object.	The lunar eclipse happens when the earth's shadow falls on the moon, thus the moon is not lit up by the sun. This happens during full moon. The solar eclipse happens when the moon passes between the earth and the sun. The moon blocks out the light from the sun. This happens during new moon.	One of two times during the year when the sun is directly over the earth's equator. At this time, the length of the day and night are nearly equal all over the world.	The Spring Equinox is called the Vernal Equinox and occurs around March 21st. The Fall Equinox is called the Autumnal Equinox and occurs around September 21st.	A large group of stars, gas and dust that contains millions to billions of stars.	Our galaxy is the Milky Way. Our sun is part of this spiral galaxy. Our galaxy has over 200 billion stars. Our sun orbits around the Milky Way Galaxy once every 250 million years.

GLOBULAR CLUSTER:	NOTES:	LIGHT YEAR:	NOTES:	LOCAL GROUP:	NOTES:
A large group of stars which is spherically shaped. It contains hundreds of thousands to a million stars or more.	There are about 150 globular clusters in the Milky Way Galaxy. They make up a halo around the disk of the Galaxy. Globular clusters are made up of very old stars and can be detected in other galaxies.	The distance that light travels in one year in a vacuum.	Light travels at a speed of 186,000 miles per second (300,000 kilometers per second) in a vacuum. A light year is six trillion miles (9.5 trillion kilometers) long.	A small cluster of galaxies of which the Milky Way is a part.	There are only two large galaxies in our local group: (1) the Milky Way and (2) Andromeda. Our local group cluster is part of a larger cluster called the "Virgo Cluster."

MAGNITUDE:	NOTES:	MAGELLANIC CLOUDS:	NOTES:	METEOR:	NOTES:
A way to tell the brightness of an astronomical object. In this system, an object is given a number for its brightness.	The lower the number in the magnitude system, the brighter the object. A first magnitude star is brighter than a third magnitude star. The human eye can only see up to sixth magnitude stars.	The two closest galaxies to us. These are satellites of our own Milky Way Galaxy.	These can be seen only from the earth's Southern Hemisphere. In the early 1500's Ferdinand Magellan's crew were the first Europeans to record these two galaxies.	A part of solid material from space that burns up in the earth's atmosphere because of friction with the air.	These are often called "shooting stars" but have nothing to do with the stars. A meteor is called a meteoroid before it enters the earth's atmosphere. When a meteoroid hits the earth it is called a meteorite.

MILKY WAY	NOTES:	MOON:	NOTES:	NEBULA:	NOTES:
A faint band of hazy light that stretches all the way around the sky.	The Milky Way is made up of a very large number of individual faint stars.	A large natural satellite of the earth.	This term is sometimes used to denote any object that orbits around a planet. Astronomers, however, prefer that the term *satellite* instead of *moon* be used.	A cloud of gas and/or dust in interstellar space.	In Latin, the word *nebula* means "cloud." The plural form of *nebula* is nebulae.

NEUTRON STAR:	NOTES:	NOVA:	NOTES:	OBSERVATORY:	NOTES:
A part left over when a huge star explodes. A rapidly spinning neutron star is called a pulsar.	Neutron stars are made up of neutron particles. A teaspoonful of neutron star material would weigh more than all the cars in the U.S. put together.	A star that suddenly but only temporarily increases its brightness.	Are thought to occur in binary stars as one star gets hotter and compressed until its material explodes.	A place in which telescopes for observing the heavens can be found.	Most observatories are located in places in high altitudes to escape light pollution from major cities.

28

ORBIT:	NOTES:	PARSEC:	NOTES:	PHASES OF THE MOON:	NOTES:
The path that one body takes as it goes around another body.	The moon orbits the earth about once every twenty-eight days. The sun orbits around the center of the Milky Way Galaxy about once every 250 million years.	A unit of distance equal to about 3.26 light years or 206,265 astronomical units.	At a distance of one parsec, the angular separation between the sun and the earth is one arc second. One arc second is equivalent to the size of a dime as seen from two miles (3 kilometers).	The difference in how the moon looks as it orbits around the earth.	There are eight phases of the moon: First Quarter, Waxing Gibbous, Full Moon, Waning Gibbous, Last Quarter, Waning Crescent, New Moon, and Waxing Crescent.

PLANET:	NOTES:	PLANETARIUM:	NOTES:	QUASAR:	NOTES:
A major object that travels around a star. A planet is a common companion of a star such as our sun.	In our solar system, there are nine planets: Mercury, Venus, Earth, Mars, Jupiter, Saturn, Uranus, Neptune and Pluto.	A domed theatre that has a projector at its center. The projector projects an image of the night sky on the dome for all to see.	In a planetarium one can generally see how the nighttime sky looks from anywhere on Earth at any time.	A faraway, extremely bright, very small object that looks like a star but really cannot be a star. Astronomers are studying how quasars produce so much light.	A quasar, in one second, produces more energy than an entire galaxy does in one second.

RADIO ASTRONOMY:	NOTES:	RED GIANT:	NOTES:	RED SHIFT:	NOTES:
A branch of astronomy in which radio waves from objects in the universe are studied.	There are only two kinds of light-like radiation that can reach the earth's surface: (1) radio waves and (2) visible light waves.	A very large, cool star, in the final stages of its life.	If our sun was a red giant, it would extend outward to the orbit of Mars. This is predicted to happen five billion years from now. Try not to worry about this happening.	The stretching of light waves coming from an object like a star that is moving away from us. A blue shift occurs when an object is moving toward us.	Astronomers believe that the universe is expanding because light from all galaxies outside our own is "red shifted," thus they are moving away from us and each other.

SECOND OF ARC:	NOTES:	S.E.T.I.:	NOTES:	SATELLITE:	NOTES:
A very small angle equal to 1/60th of a minute of arc which is 1/60th of a degree.	A line across the sky from horizon to horizon on Earth equals 180°. The diameter of a dime seen at two miles (3 kilometers) has a diameter of a second of arc.	Initials that mean "Search for Extra-Terrestrial Intelligence."	At this time, astronomers are searching to find radio waves transmitted from outer space by others.	An object that orbits around another larger one. Callisto is a satellite of the planet Jupiter.	The earth's natural satellite is called "moon." Some satellites that orbit the earth are called "artificial satellites."

SOLAR SYSTEM:	NOTES:	SOLSTICE:	NOTES:	SPECTRUM:	NOTES:
The sun, nine major planets, satellites, asteroids, and comets that orbit around the sun.	The solar system is only a very small part of the universe.	Two times during the year when the sun seen from earth is seen at its farthest point north or south of the equator.	The summer solstice occurs when the sun is over the Tropic of Cancer on June 21st, the first day of summer. The winter solstice occurs when the sun is over the Tropic of Capricorn on December 21st, the first day of winter.	A band of colors from red to violet that occurs as a result of passing white light through a prism.	The band of colors from red to violet can be remembered by the code name "Roy G. Biv," red, orange, yellow, green, blue, indigo and violet.

STAR:	NOTES:	STAR CLUSTER:	NOTES:	SUN:	NOTES:
A large hot ball of gas. A star gets its energy from a nuclear reaction in its core.	Our sun is a very good example of a star.	A group of stars that hold each other together by their own gravity.	The two kinds of star clusters in the Milky Way Galaxy are the younger galactic star clusters and the older globular clusters.	The sun is a star that is located at the center of our solar system.	We depend on the sun to maintain life on Earth.

SUPERNOVA:	NOTES:	TELESCOPE:	NOTES:	UNIVERSE:	NOTES:
An explosion that occurs at the end of a very large star's life.	An exploding supernova star, can outshine all other stars in the galaxy for several days. It then cools, leaving behind a crushed core.	An instrument that gathers light or other radiation and brings it into focus so it can be analyzed.	The "size" of a telescope refers to how large the light-gathering area of the telescope actually is.	To an astronomer the universe is the sum total of all observable things or objects whose physical efforts on other things can be detected.	The universe is infinitely larger than our solar system.

VARIABLE STAR:	NOTES:	WHITE DWARF:	NOTES:	ANALEMMA:	NOTES:
A special kind of star that changes its brightness.	As an amateur astronomer, you may make an important discovery in astronomy by observing the actions of a variable star.	A collapsed part of a low mass star that has spent all its nuclear fuel and shines only by radiating away its stored up heat.	Our sun will become a white dwarf at the end of its life five billion years from now.	An analemma shows the position of the sun and its latitude every day of the year.	An analemma can sometimes be found on a globe. It looks like this:

OVERHEAD PROJECTOR PLASTIC PLANETARIUM NIGHT SKY

You will need an 8″ x 8″ (20 cm x 20 cm) piece of thick plastic, pushpins, tape, scissors and some scrap cardboard. Make a copy of the sky map below. Cut out sky map. Tape sky map faceup to plastic. Tape the edges to hold sky map in place. Pin sky map with attached plastic to thick cardboard. With a pushpin, punch a hole through sky map and attached plastic at each dot (star). Separate plastic from sky map. Place plastic on overhead projector. Project image on screen. Have students identify the constellations shown by the plastic night sky. Names of constellations are found on the original sky map below.

 TIP: A corn skewer with one of two prongs removed, ice pick or sharp point of a compass can also be used to punch holes in the plastic. Proceed slowly and carefully while making your planetarium night sky. Polystyrene plastic with a thickness of .020 inch works well for this overhead planetarium.

PLASTIC BUBBLE PLANETARIUM

You will need two 6 mil 10′ x 25′ (3 m x 8 m) sheets of Visqueen plastic or 4 mm clear polyethylene film, tape, scissors, and a 3-speed electric fan. Fold plastic in half. Hold upright in middle and tape edges to the floor with tape. Cut a 24″ (60 cm) slit at the fold for an entrance. Make a 24″ (60 cm) hole in one end. Tape plastic to fan to feed the flow of air from fan into the bubble.

Turn fan on to inflate bubble. Have students enter bubble. Project celestial bodies onto walls and ceiling using flashlights or slide projectors. Observe shapes from both inside and outside of bubble. Have students make sketches of what they see. Add cardboard fins to outside of bubble to make a spaceship. With accompanying music, take an imaginary trip to outer space. Have students record their feelings in a science log.

 TIP: Be sure plastic is firmly taped to the floor and bubble; when inflated, it will be tall enough for students to enter and exit easily. Have students remove shoes when entering the bubble. The fan remains on at all times. Reverse slides in slide projector tray if students inside bubble view slides projected from outside bubble by slide projector. Images are reversed. Use different colored slides made of cellophane paper to project various colors onto bubble. Use black lights for futuristic illusion. Add recorded sound effects for various astronomical themes.

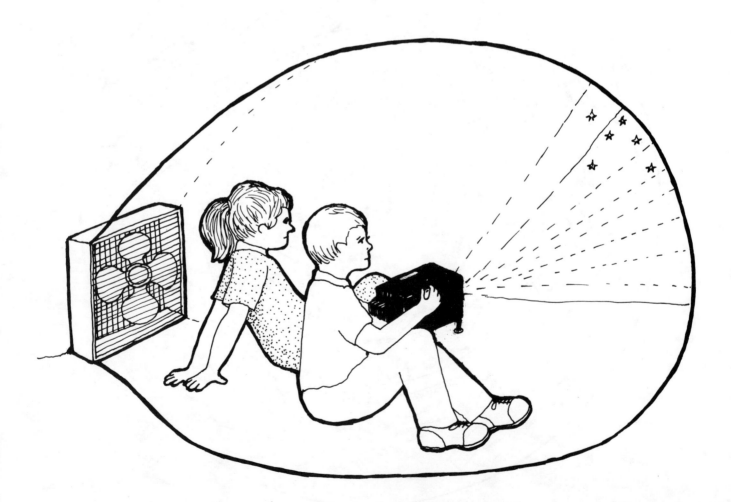

STAR SAMPLING DEVICE

You will need scissors, cardboard and laminating machine if available. Make a copy of this page. Cut out small square on the solid lines. Cut inside square on dotted lines to make a frame with a one-square-inch opening. This is a completed sampling device. Have students drop frame anywhere on the sky below. Count the number of stars inside the 1″ frame. Have students multiply by 36 to determine the approximate number of stars in the sky without counting each individual star.

 TIP: Mount the 1″ squares on single-layered cardboard. Cut out 1″ square. Laminate the star sampling device for lasting durability. The lamination becomes a window to view the stars within the 1″ opening.

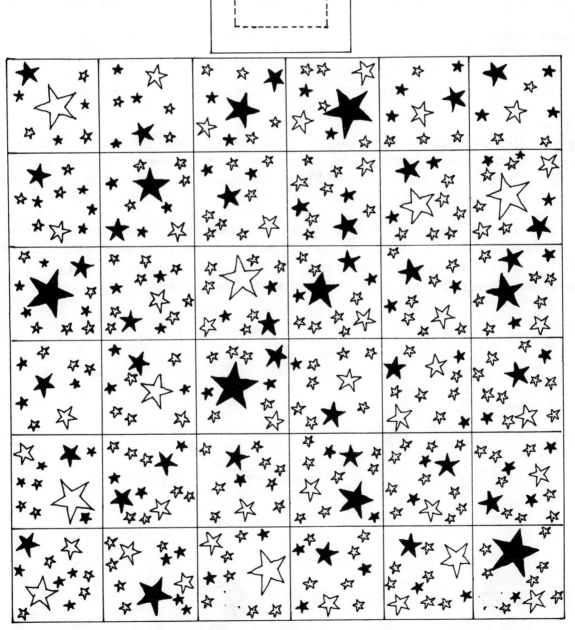

SEASONAL SKY CHARTS, TRANSPARENCIES AND/OR COPYMASTERS

Background Information: This section features a series of seven sets of paired seasonal sky charts. The sky is divided conveniently into six seasonal charts. The seventh chart features a pair of circumpolar constellation pages. The approximate local times for use of the six seasonal charts are as follows:

Early Fall		**Easter**	
August 1	11:30 p.m.	March 1	11:30 p.m.
August 15	10:30 p.m.	March 15	10:30 p.m.
August 30	9:30 p.m.	March 30	9:30 p.m.

Late Fall		**Spring**	
October 1	11:30 p.m.	April 1	11:30 p.m.
October 15	10:30 p.m.	April 15	10:30 p.m.
October 30	9:30 p.m.	April 30	9:30 p.m.

Early Winter		**Summer**	
December 1	11:30 p.m.	June 1	11:30 p.m.
December 15	10:30 p.m.	June 15	10:30 p.m.
December 30	9:30 p.m.	June 30	9:30 p.m.

 TIP: The charts can be used at other times during the year. For instance, the early winter chart can be used during a January evening any time between 7:30 p.m. and 9:30 p.m. The early fall chart can be used in the month of July between 1:30 a.m. on the first of July until 11:30 p.m. on the thirty-first of July.

Each of the following paired charts are set up so that the east and west points on the horizon are represented by the middle of the left and right-hand side of the paper, respectively. The southern point is exactly in the middle of the page at the bottom. The observer's horizon is a gradually curving line through the east, south and west points. The diagram below represents this point.

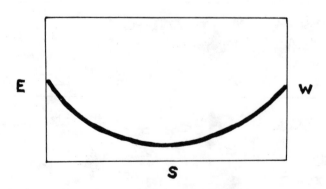

Figure 1

Each of the six paired seasonal sky charts is drawn so the observer who uses them initially faces south. The observer should note that the constellations near the north celestial pole, marked by the star Polaris (see page 37), are in some cases distorted from their actual size and shape. This is because a spherical surface, such as the celestial sphere, is drawn on a flat two-dimensional surface. The user should also notice that all circumpolar constellations are not drawn on each chart. Because the observer is assumed to be facing south, any part of the sky well behind the observer would be difficult to see. A seventh paired chart, a circumpolar chart, is included specifically for those observations when one faces *north*. These circumpolar charts, found on pages 36 and 37, can be used all year long.

Because of the observer's latitude on earth, there are areas in the sky in which the stars never rise or set, but just seem to circle the pole star. The circumpolar sky for latitude + 40° North lies within the large circle on the chart. To use the chart at any time during the year, the observer should rotate the chart in the desired direction until the patterns in the sky match the orientation of those on the chart.

 TIP: A pair of pages for each of the six seasonal sky charts are included for your use. The second page in each set, the teacher page, has the *names* of major constellations and stars appropriately labeled. The first page, the student page, has dots for the stars but names to represent the stars are omitted.

The seasonal sky charts can be reproduced and given to each student one chart at a time according to the time of the year. In this way, observation and interest for what is visible in the sky will continue throughout the entire school year. In addition, you may want to make transparencies of the circumpolar and seasonal sky charts. Place on overhead projector. Identify constellations according to various seasons of the year.

CIRCUMPOLAR TRANSPARENCY
AND/OR COPYMASTER

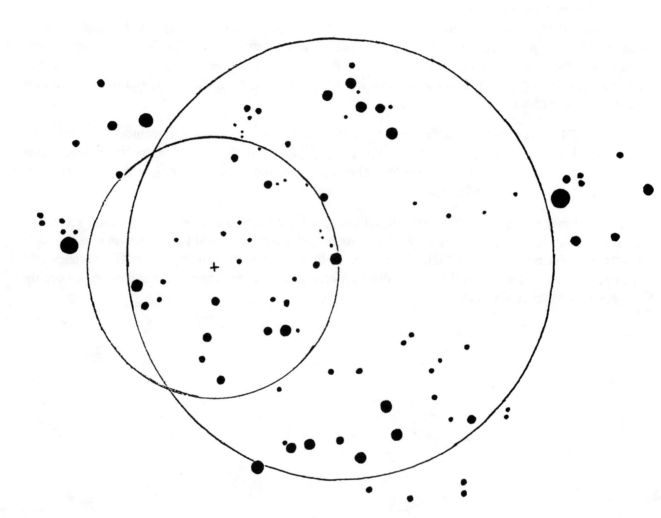

Circumpolar Sky

CIRCUMPOLAR TRANSPARENCY
AND/OR COPYMASTER

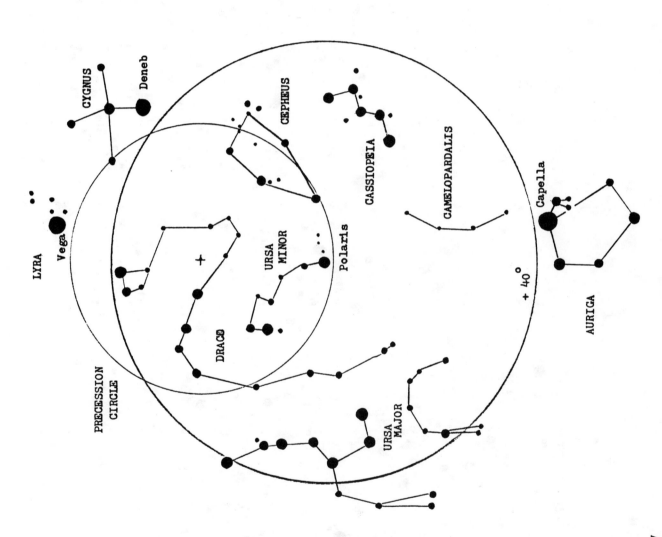

KEY: Circumpolar Sky

Early Fall Sky

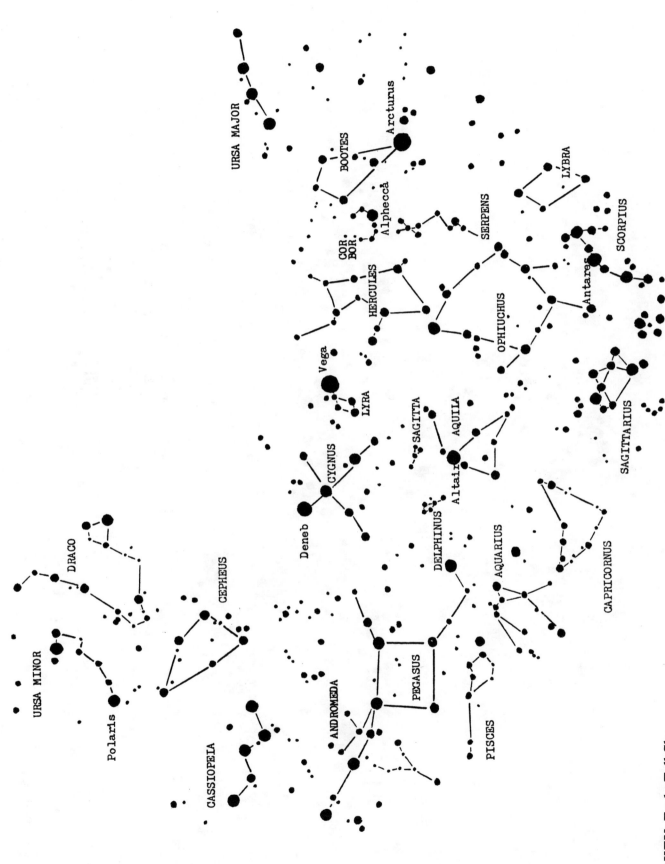

KEY: Early Fall Sky

Late Fall Sky

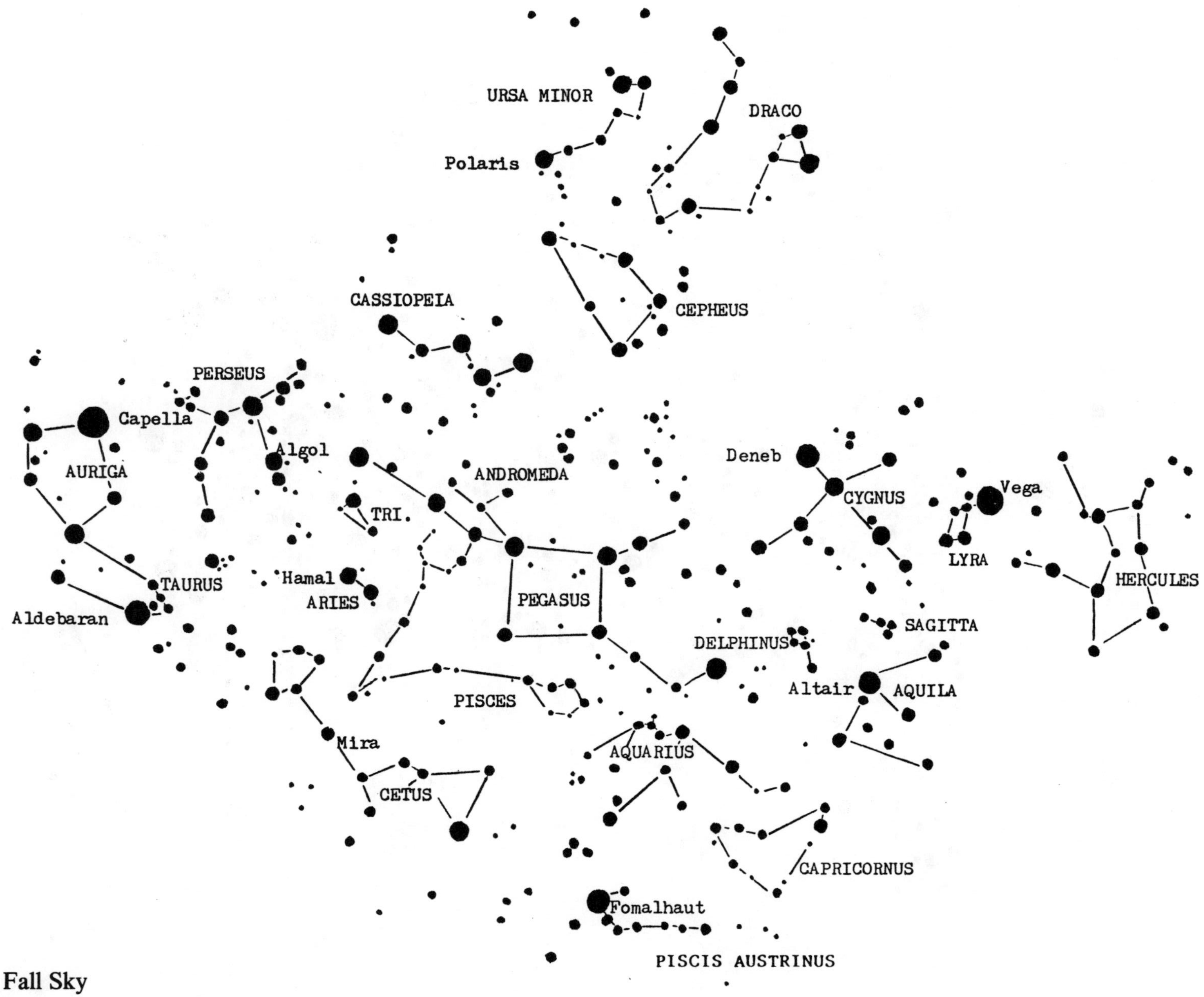

KEY: Late Fall Sky

41

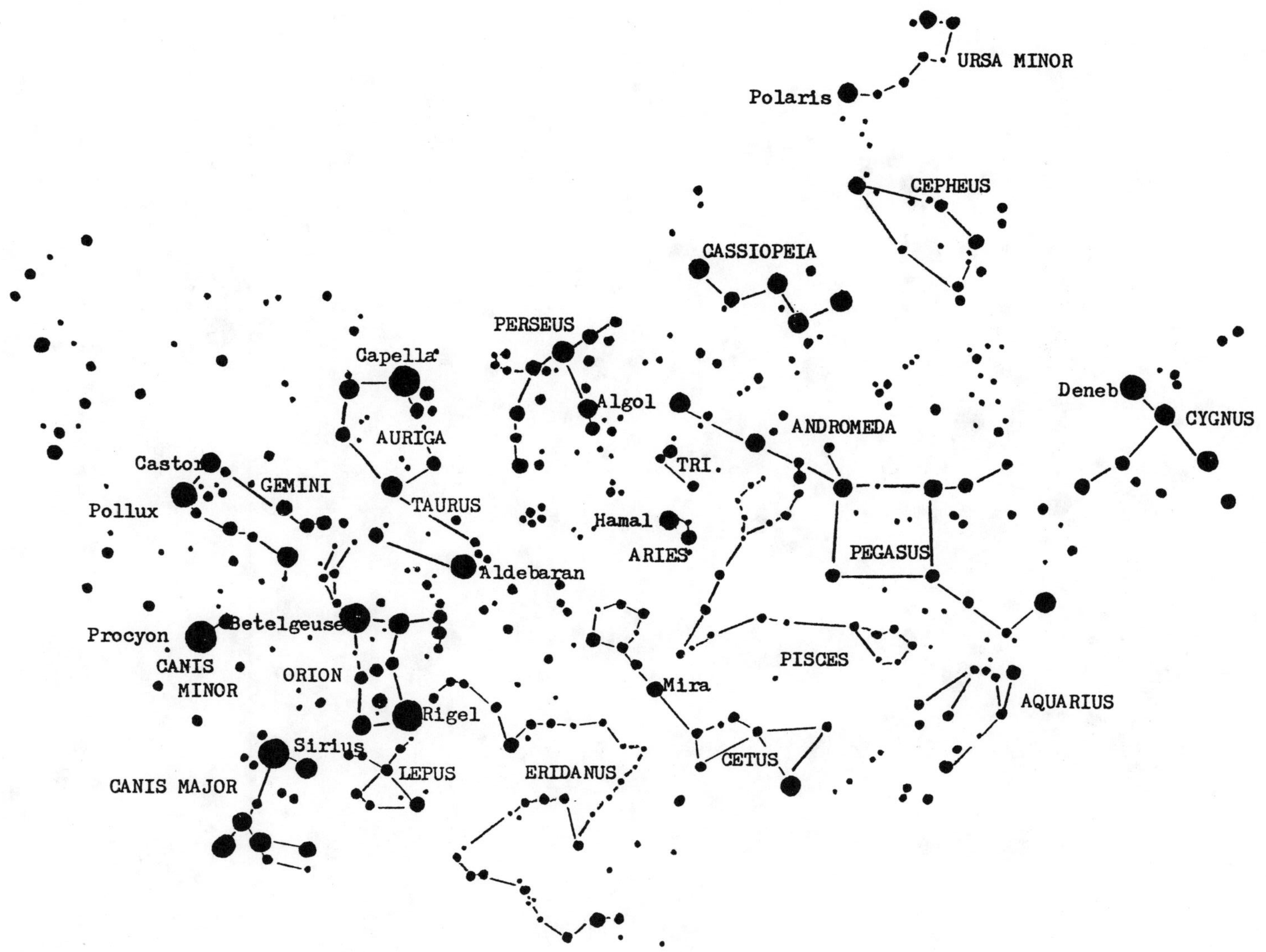

KEY: Early Winter Sky

43

KEY: Easter Sky

45

Spring Sky

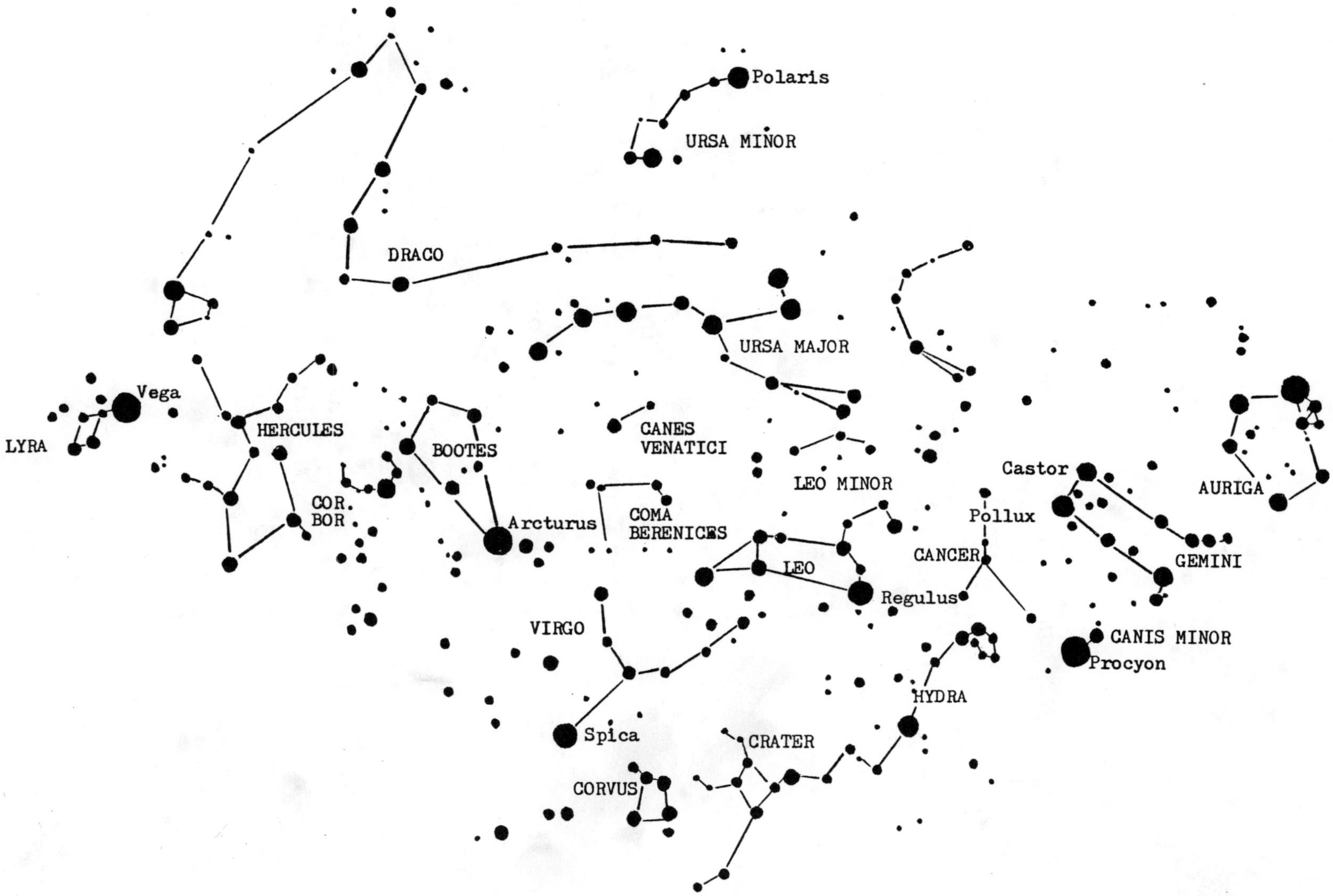

KEY: Spring Sky

AURIGA

GEMINI

CANIS MINOR
Procyon

Castor
Pollux

CANCER

Regulus

HYDRA

LEO MINOR

LEO

CRATER

URSA MAJOR

Polaris
URSA MINOR

CANES
VENATICI

COMA
BERENICES

CORVUS

Spica

VIRGO

Arcturus

BOOTES

DRACO

COR.
BOR.

HERCULES

Vega

LYRA

KEY: Summer Sky

49

HOW TO USE SEASONAL SKY CHARTS, TRANSPARENCIES AND/OR COPYMASTERS

Use of Guidepost Constellations

The reader who uses the seasonal sky charts will note that several constellations can be used as guideposts to find other constellations. Once a particular constellation is identified, it is easy to locate other star patterns in the area. For example, when using the Spring Sky seasonal sky chart (see page 53), one notes the guidepost constellation Ursa Major, or more popularly known as the Big Bear.* A line drawn through the two pointer stars (Merak and Dubhe) that form the side of the bowl farthest from the handle in the Big Dipper in Ursa Major will point to the North Star, Polaris, which in turn marks the end of the handle of the Little Dipper or Ursa Minor (see Figure 2). The two stars, Merak and Dubhe, are called pointer stars. The diagram below shows the location of Merak and Dubhe, the pointer stars in the Big Dipper.

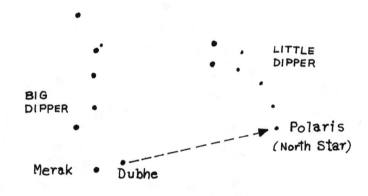

Figure 2

In the spring, the Big Dipper can also be used to locate several other constellations. A line drawn southward, or backwards, through the pointer stars leads to the back of Leo, the Lion, the backwards question mark (see page 53). The Big Dipper can also be used to locate the two major spring constellations, Bootes and its bright star Arcturus and Virgo with its prominent star Spica. One merely imagines a line that curves along the handle of the Big Dipper through the star Alcaid and onto the orange star Arcturus. Continuing the curved line southward about the same distance as Arcturus is from Alcaid, you will spot Alpha Virginis or the white star Spica. These lines, drawn on the spring sky chart, are found on page 53. Finding Bootes and Virgo in the same manner will

---

*Astronomers agree that the Big Dipper is not a constellation by itself; rather the Big Dipper is part of a constellation called Ursa Major, the Big Bear.

lead to two other constellations. Just to the east of Bootes is a faint semicircle of stars. These dim stars form the constellation Corona Borealis, the Northern Crown. To the south and west of Virgo are four stars that make the constellation Corvus, the Crow.

When using the winter seasonal sky chart (see page 54), one can use Orion the Great Hunter as a guidepost constellation. Once Orion is found, it is easy to locate at least six other constellations in the immediate vicinity.

Orion is a rectangularly shaped constellation with four bright stars that mark its corners. The center of the rectangle in Orion is marked by three bright stars that lie nearly in a straight line. These stars make up Orion's belt. Figure 3 below shows the familiar shape of Orion.

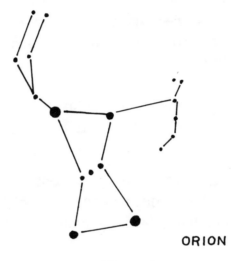

ORION

Figure 3

The stars in the belt of Orion point to the northwest in the direction of Aldebaran, the bright orange star of Taurus, the Bull. The head of the bull is marked by a cluster of stars in the shape of a "V." The cluster is known as the Hyades (see page 54).

Using Orion again, but this time pointing to the southeast, one finds Sirius, the brightest star in the entire sky. Sirius is the Dog star and marks the position of the constellation of Canis Major, the Big Dog. Orion's other hunting dog, Canis Minor with its bright star Procyon, is just as easy to find as Sirius. A line drawn through the shoulder stars of Orion, Bellatrix and Betelgeuse eastward leads the eye to Procyon and the Little Dog. Procyon, together with Sirius and Betelgeuse, form an equilateral triangle that covers a large portion of the winter sky (see page 54).

Orion can be used to find other constellations. Starting in the southwest part of the rectangle marked by the bright star Rigel, follow a line through Betelgeuse to the northeast (see page 54). The line will point the way to Gemini, the Twins. The heads of the twins are marked by two first magnitude stars, Pollux and Castor, both of which act as guidepost stars. A line from Castor through Pollux points in the general direction of the dim constellation of Cancer, the Crab.

There are two other constellations that can be found when using Orion as a guidepost constellation. Over Orion's head lies the pentagon-shaped pattern of stars called Auriga (see page 54). Its bright star, Capella, is easy to spot during the winter because it lies directly overhead when at its highest point above the horizon. To the south of Orion and difficult to observe from the city because of light pollution, is Lepus, the Hare. To the west of Orion is the long winding constellation of Eridanus, the River.

Constellations that are visible at other times of the year can act as further road maps in the sky. The great square of Pegasus is an excellent place to start when attempting to locate fall constellations (see page 55). In the Summer Triangle, locate the triangle marked by the stars Deneb, Vega and Altair which serve as guideposts to the summer (see page 56).

Locating constellations is an easy and enjoyable task. Once your students identify certain patterns in the sky, their interest will be heightened. In turn, they will develop an appreciation for, and a greater understanding of, the vast universe in which we live.

 TIP: Make transparencies from guidepost constellations pages 53-56. Place on an overhead projector. Walk your students through the spring, summer, fall and winter skies by following the paths designated by arrows on the pages.

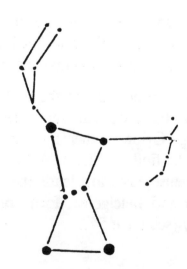

GUIDEPOST CONSTELLATIONS: THE SPRING SKY

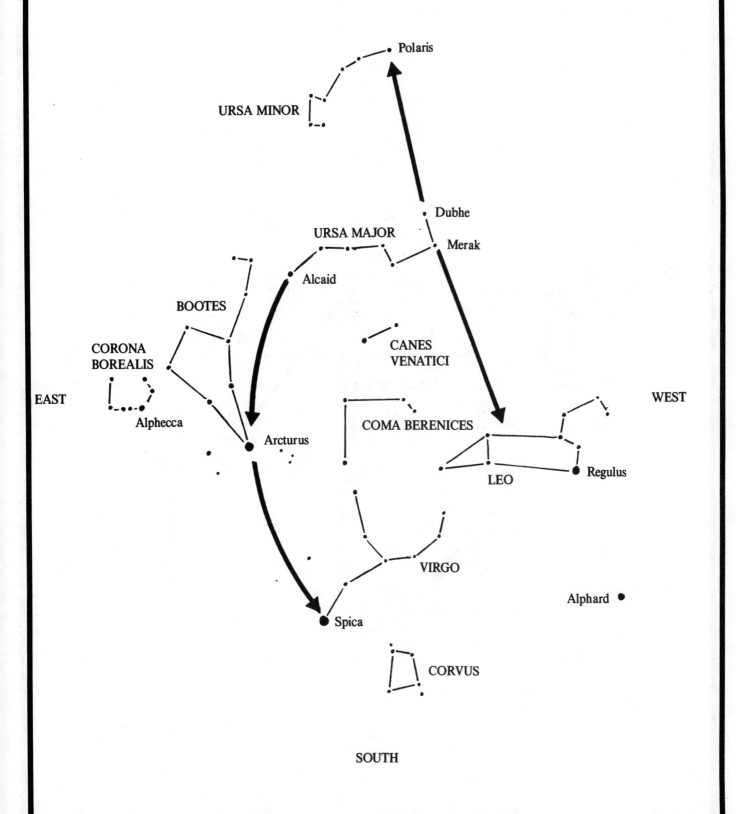

EAST

WEST

SOUTH

GUIDEPOST CONSTELLATIONS: THE WINTER TRIANGLE

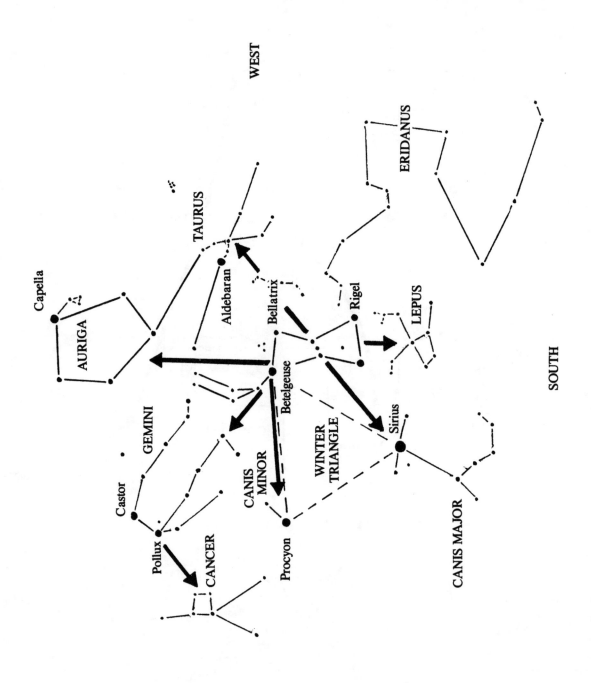

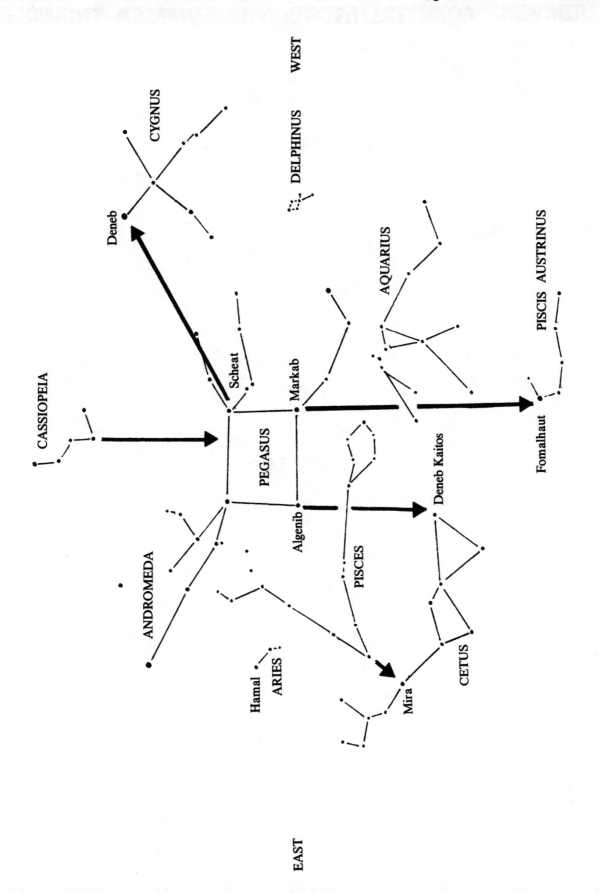

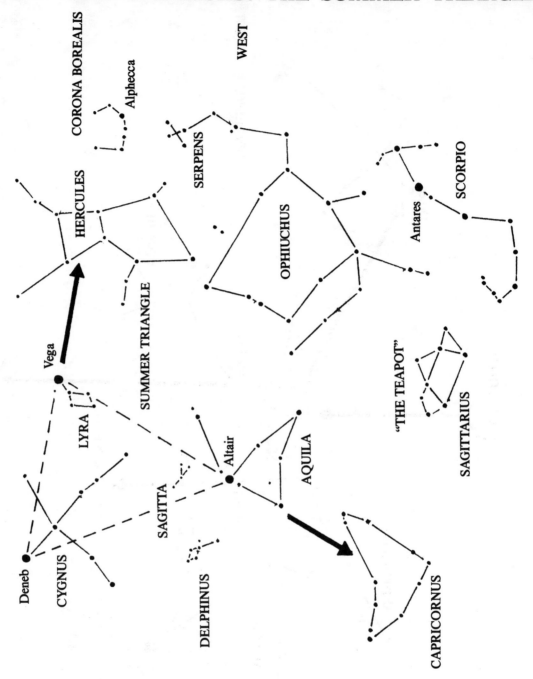

FOLD-OUT WALL SKY CHART OF CONSTELLATIONS

To help students learn where various constellations are related to each other in the night sky, make copies of this handy fold-out wall sky chart of constellations. This chart was made by replotting each constellation found on the copymasters in this book (see pages 84-118) to scale on a large sheet of paper. Constellations were plotted with the same information and in their respective locations relative to one another. The chart, reproduced at one-half scale, is found on the following pages and may be copied for student use. You will notice that the chart is divided into two major sections: (1) the northern, southern and equatorial constellations are plotted in one long rectangular area and (2) the portion of the sky that is continuously visible from + 30° N latitude is plotted in a second circular section. The purpose for plotting the north circumpolar constellations with a circular scale is to minimize any distortion that would occur as a result of plotting a spherical surface on a flat two-dimensional sheet of paper.

The fold-out wall sky chart is made to show students the relative positions of the constellations in the sky. In addition, the sky chart has another use. Small colored spheres that represent the sun, moon and five visible planets can be placed on the map according to their yearly positions in the sky. As various objects move in the sky, corresponding spheres can be moved accordingly. In the case of the moon and its changing phases, eight small circles can be drawn with the various phases of the moon represented. These circles can be moved daily as the phase and position of the moon change with respect to the distant stars. Make a copy of the fold-out wall sky chart for each student. Enjoy looking to the sky.

 TIP: To assemble the chart, merely place one tab from one page over the next page. Slide pages together until figures meet. Tape or glue pages together. Laminate for lasting durability.

FOLD-OUT WALL SKY CHART

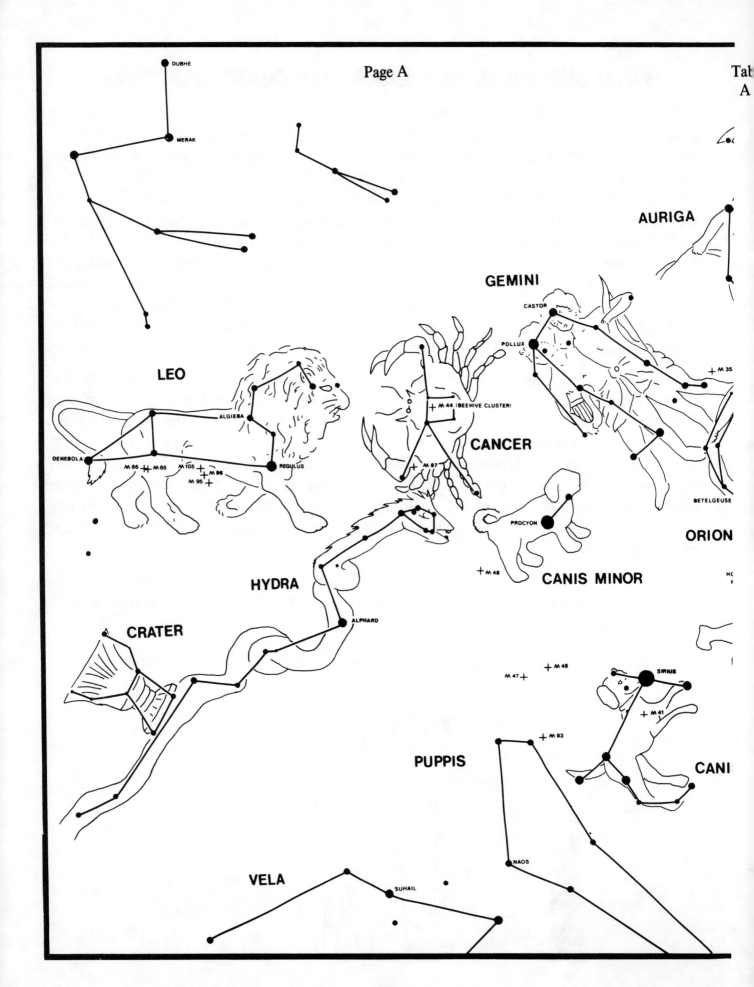

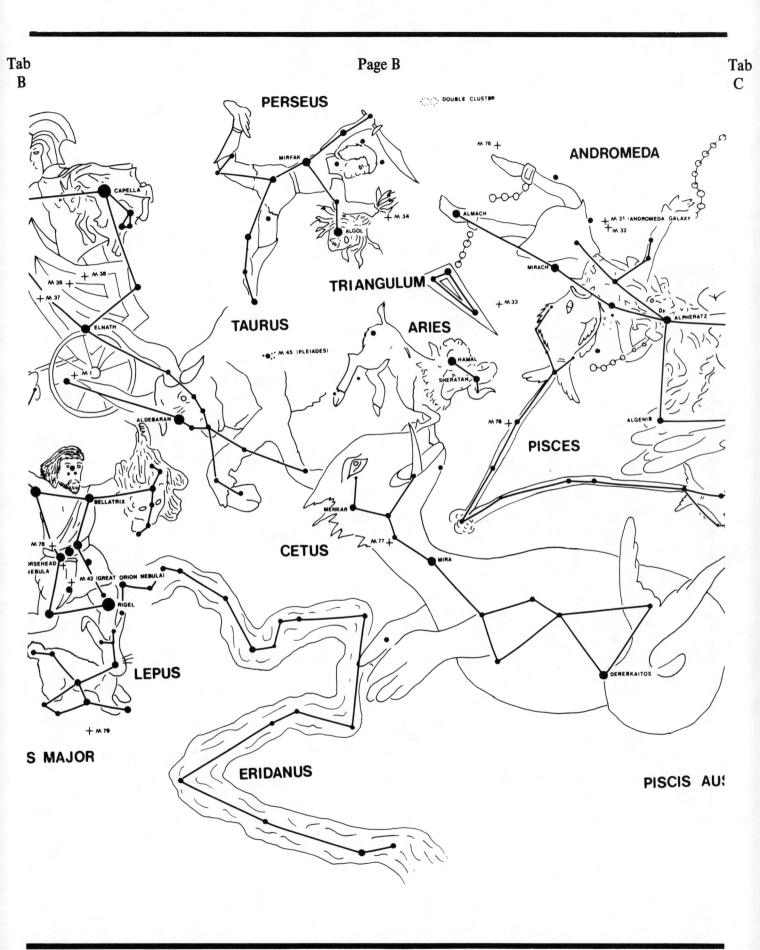

DOUBLE CLUSTER

PERSEUS

ANDROMEDA

M 76 +

MIRFAK

M 31 (ANDROMEDA GALAXY)
ALMACH
M 32 +

M 34 +

ALGOL

MIRACH

TRIANGULUM

TAURUS

ARIES

M 33 +

ALPHERATZ

HAMAL

M 45 (PLEIADES)

SHERATAN

CAPELLA

M 38 +
M 36 +
M 37 +

ELNATH

M 1

ALDEBARAN

M 74 +

PISCES

ALGENIB

BELLATRIX

MENKAR

M 77 +

CETUS

MIRA

M 78 +

HORSEHEAD
NEBULA

M 42 (GREAT ORION NEBULA)

RIGEL

LEPUS

M 79 +

S MAJOR

DENEBKAITOS

ERIDANUS

PISCIS AUS

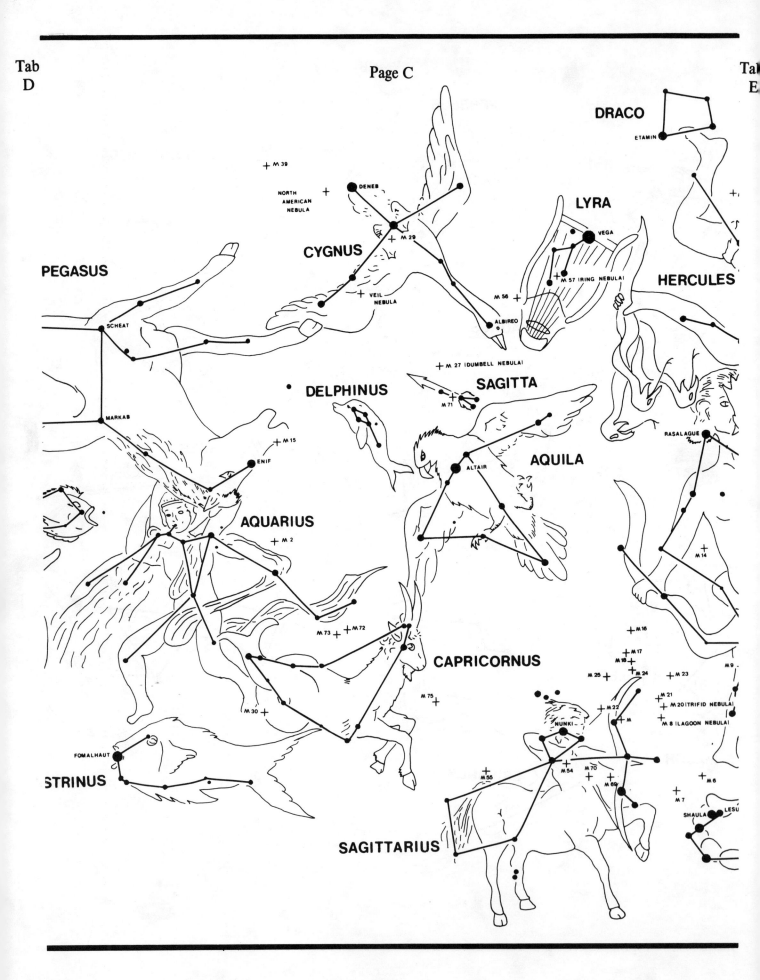

DRACO

ETAMIN

+ M 39

NORTH
AMERICAN
NEBULA

DENEB

LYRA

VEGA

CYGNUS

M 57 (RING NEBULA)

HERCULES

VEIL
NEBULA

M 56

ALBIREO

PEGASUS

SCHEAT

+ M 27 (DUMBELL NEBULA)

DELPHINUS

SAGITTA

M 71

MARKAB

RASALAGUE

+ M 15

ENIF

AQUILA

ALTAIR

AQUARIUS

+ M 2

M 14

M 16

+ M 17

M 18

M 24

M 25

M 23

M 9

M 73 + M 72

CAPRICORNUS

M 21

M 20 (TRIFID NEBULA)

M 8 (LAGOON NEBULA)

M 75

M 22

M

M 30

FOMALHAUT

NUNKI

M 55

M 54

M 70

M 69

M 6

M 7

STRINUS

SHAULA

LESU

SAGITTARIUS

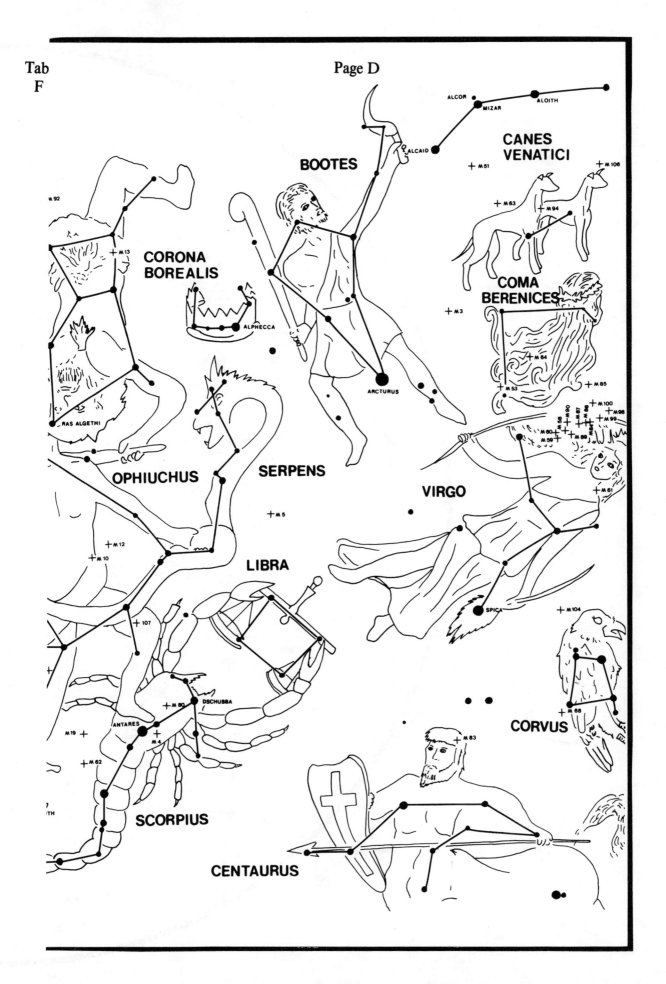

CANES
VENATICI

+ M51

+ M106

+ M63   + M94

BOOTES

M 92

CORONA
BOREALIS

+ M13

COMA
BERENICES

+ M3

ALPHECCA

+ M64

RAS ALGETHI

+ M53   + M85

+ M100
+ M58
M90   + M98
M87   + M99
M60   M84
M59   M86

SERPENS

OPHIUCHUS

ARCTURUS

VIRGO

+M5

+ M12

+ M61

+ M10

LIBRA

SPICA

+ M104

+ 107

ANTARES

DSCHUBBA

+ M68

+ M80

CORVUS

M 19 +

+ M4

+ M83

+ M 62

SCORPIUS

CENTAURUS

ALCOR   ALOITH
MIZAR

ALCAID

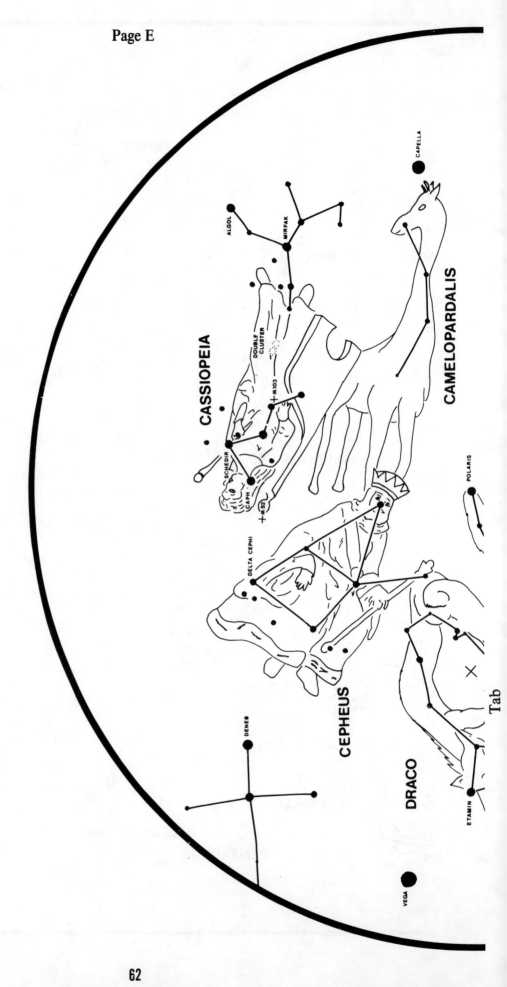

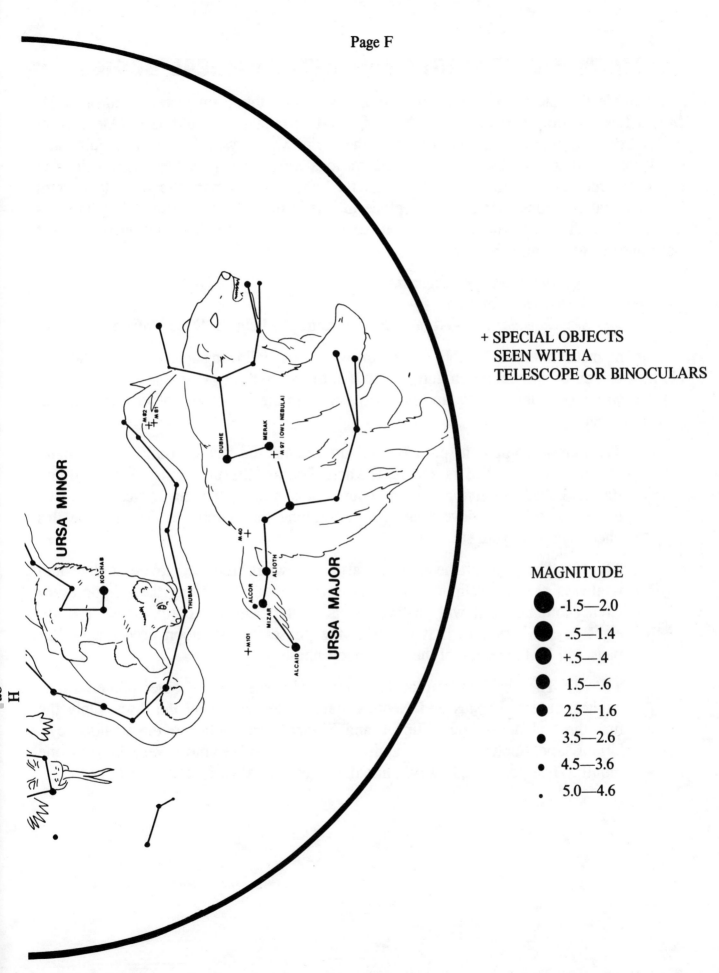

+ SPECIAL OBJECTS
SEEN WITH A
TELESCOPE OR BINOCULARS

URSA MINOR

URSA MAJOR

KOCHAB

THUBAN

DUBHE

MERAK

M 97 (OWL NEBULA)

M 82

M 81

M 40

M101

ALCOR

MIZAR

ALIOTH

ALCAID

MAGNITUDE

-1.5—2.0

-.5—1.4

+.5—.4

1.5—.6

2.5—1.6

3.5—2.6

4.5—3.6

5.0—4.6

MAGNETIC PATHWAYS FOR ASTRONOMICAL BODIES

Assemble the fold-out wall sky chart of constellations found on pages 58 through 63. Mount this fold-out chart on a thin sheet of metal or magnetic chalkboard. (Metal from a discarded dishwasher, refrigerator or clothes drier works well for this.) Acquire and label colored magnetic discs that represent various astronomical bodies. Attach discs to sky chart mounted on the metal or magnetic board. Move magnetic discs to current astronomical positions. Lift off and replace magnetic discs for each succeeding month's display. Consult one of the following sources of information for information on current positions of astronomical bodies:

> *Sky and Telescope Magazine*
> *Astronomy Magazine*
> *Sky Calendar* from Abrams Planetarium at Michigan State University

This magnetic board is suitable for the display of the following astronomical features: (1) the position of the sun, moon and planets, (2) the path of any visible artificial satellite, (3) the motion of visible comets and (4) the position in the sky of any other astronomical object or event.

 TIP (1): The apparent path of the sun around the sky is confined to a band of constellations called the *zodiac.* The actual path of the sun against the background stars is called the *ecliptic.* In the course of a month, the sun moves about 30° along the ecliptic. Move magnetic discs along the ecliptic to demonstrate this phenomenon to your students.

 TIP (2): The path of the moon is also somewhat restricted to the zodiac and is always near the ecliptic. The moon moves about 13° along the ecliptic every twenty-four hours. It will go through its eight phases in approximately twenty-eight days. Move discs that represent the phases of the moon accordingly. See page 149 for the names of the eight moon phases.

 TIP (3): The positions of planets, particularly those of the outer planets Mars, Jupiter, Saturn, Uranus and Neptune can be designated by the discs. Only the first three planets—Mars, Jupiter and Saturn—are visible to the unaided eye. Uranus and Neptune, which require a telescope to see, move very little in one month. Their positions, however, like the moon, are always near the ecliptic.

CARD DECKS OF CONSTELLATIONS

You will need copies of the following four pages, scissors, laminating machine and magnetic tape if available. Make copies of the four pages. If possible, laminate the pages. Have students cut out the cards that feature scientific names for the eighty-eight constellations. Cut out the eighty-eight matching common name cards. Make two decks of cards. Have students play concentration games matching names of those constellations found in Card Deck A with those found in answer Card Deck B.

 TIP: For easy-to-use answer key, merely mount page B, the answer card page, to the back of page A which features the scientific names of the constellations. The scientific name cards and common name answer cards are back to back. Laminate for lasting durability. Use often. Enjoy.

CARD DECK A

1 ANDROMEDA	2 ANTILLA	3 APUS	4 AQUARIUS	5 AQUILA	6 ARA
7 ARIES	8 AURIGA	9 BOOTES	10 CAELUM	11 CAMELOPAR-DALIS	12 CANCER
13 CANES VENATICI	14 CANIS MAJOR	15 CANIS MINOR	16 CAPRICORNUS	17 CARINA	18 CASSIOPEIA
19 CENTAURUS	20 CEPHEUS	21 CETUS	22 CHAMAELEON	23 CIRCINUS	24 COLUMBA
25 COMA BERENICES	26 CORONA AUSTRINA	27 CORONA BOREALIS	28 CORVUS	29 CRATER	30 CRUX
31 CYGNUS	32 DELPHINUS	33 DORADO	34 DRACO	35 EQUULEUS	36 ERIDANUS
37 FORNAX	38 GEMINI	39 GRUS	40 HERCULES	41 HOROLOGIUM	42 HYDRA

CARD DECK A

43 HYDRUS	44 INDUS	45 LACERTA	46 LEO	47 LEO MINOR	48 LEPUS
49 LIBRA	50 LUPUS	51 LYNX	52 LYRA	53 MENSA	54 MICRO-SCOPIUM
55 MONOCEROS	56 MUSCA	57 NORMA	58 OCTANS	59 OPHIUCHUS	60 ORION
61 PAVO	62 PEGASUS	63 PERSEUS	64 PHOENIX	65 PICTOR	66 PISCES
67 PISCIS AUSTRINUS	68 PUPPIS	69 PYXIS	70 RETICULUM	71 SAGITTA	72 SAGITTARIUS
73 SCORPIUS	74 SCULPTOR	75 SCUTUM	76 SERPENS	77 SEXTANS	78 TAURUS
79 TELESCOPIUM	80 TRIANGULUM	81 TRIANGULUM AUSTRALE	82 TUCANA	83 URSA MINOR	84 URSA MINOR
85 VELA	86 VIRGO	87 VOLANS	88 VULPECULA		

CARD DECK B

6A THE ALTAR	**5A** THE EAGLE	**4A** THE WATER BEARER	**3A** THE BIRD OF PARADISE	**2A** THE AIR PUMP	**1A** PRINCESS OF ETHIOPIA
12A THE CRAB	**11A** THE GIRAFFE	**10A** THE SCULPTOR'S CHISEL	**9A** THE HERDSMAN	**8A** THE CHARIOTEER	**7A** THE RAM
18A THE QUEEN OF ETHIOPIA	**17A** THE KEEL (OF ARGO NAVIS)	**16A** THE SEA GOAT	**15A** THE LITTLE DOG	**14A** THE BIG DOG	**13A** THE HUNTING DOGS
24A THE DOVE (OF NOAH)	**23A** THE COMPASS	**22A** THE CHAMELEON	**21A** THE WHALE MONSTER	**20A** KING OF ETHIOPIA	**19A** THE CENTAUR
30A THE SOUTHERN CROSS	**29A** THE CUP	**28A** THE CROW	**27A** THE NORTHERN CROWN	**26A** THE SOUTHERN CROWN	**25A** BERENICE'S HAIR
36A THE RIVER	**35A** THE FOAL	**34A** THE DRAGON	**33A** THE SWORDFISH	**32A** THE DOLPHIN	**31A** THE SWAN
42A THE SEA SERPENT	**41A** THE CLOCK	**40A** SON OF ZEUS	**39A** THE CRANE	**38A** THE TWINS	**37A** THE LABORATORY FURNACE

CARD DECK B

48A THE HARE	47A THE LION CLUB	46A THE LION	45A THE LIZARD	44A THE AMERICAN INDIAN	43A THE WATER SNAKE
54A THE MICROSCOPE	53A THE TABLE MOUNTAIN	52A THE HARP	51A THE LYNX	50A THE WOLF	49A THE SCALES
60A THE GREAT HUNTER	59A THE SERPENT HOLDER	58A THE OCTANT	57A THE CARPENTER'S SQUARE	56A THE FLY	55A THE UNICORN
66A THE FISH	65A THE PAINTER'S EASEL	64A THE PHOENIX	63A THE HERO	62A THE FLYING HORSE	61A THE PEACOCK
72A THE ARCHER	71A THE ARROW	70A THE NET	69A THE COMPASS BOX (OF ARGO NAVIS)	68A THE STERN (OF ARGO NAVIS)	67A THE SOUTHERN FISH
78A THE BULL	77A THE SEXTANT	76A THE SERPENT	75A THE SHIELD	74A THE SCULPTOR'S WORKSHOP	73A THE SCORPION
84A THE LITTLE BEAR	83A THE BIG BEAR	82A THE TOUCAN	81A THE SOUTHERN TRIANGLE	80A THE TRIANGLE	79A THE TELESCOPE
		88A THE FOX	87A THE FLYING FISH	86A THE VIRGIN	85A THE SAIL (OF ARGO NAVIS)

CONSTELLATION BOOKLETS

This page features two mini constellation booklets. You can make many more. When folded on the dotted lines, these handy booklets feature the constellation on the front cover with matching figure on the back cover. Make copies of the booklets for your students. Have students cut out and fold the booklets. Students then open booklets and write information about the constellation and matching figure inside the booklets. Laminate for safekeeping.

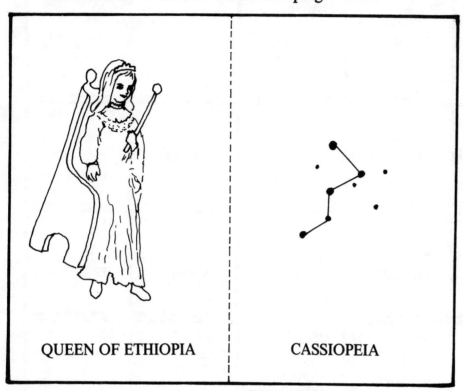

QUEEN OF ETHIOPIA | CASSIOPEIA

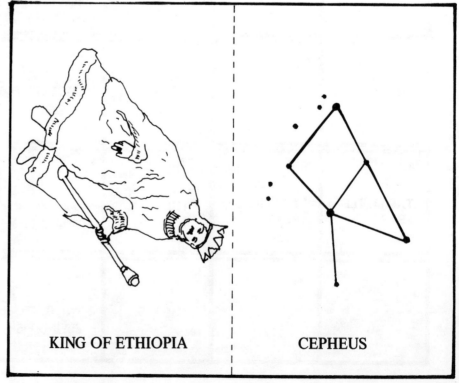

KING OF ETHIOPIA | CEPHEUS

CHANGING CONSTELLATION BULLETIN BOARD: PRESENT TO 100,000 YEARS

You will need a bulletin board covered with paper, overhead projector, marking pens, pins or stapler. Make copies of the following two pages. Cut out each constellation. Mount on index cards. Print names of constellations on backs of index cards. Laminate for lasting durability. Label bulletin board "The Changing Constellations" as shown below. Divide bulletin board in half. Mark one side "As Seen Today," the other side "As Seen in 100,000 Years." Have students pin matching constellations on correct half of bulletin board. Note changes in constellation figures over the years.

 TIP: Make a transparency of each of the pages. Place transparency on overhead projector. Project image onto bulletin board. Trace images onto paper that covers bulletin board. Move overhead projector closer to the bulletin board for smaller images, farther away for larger images. Identify each constellation and observe how it changes over time.

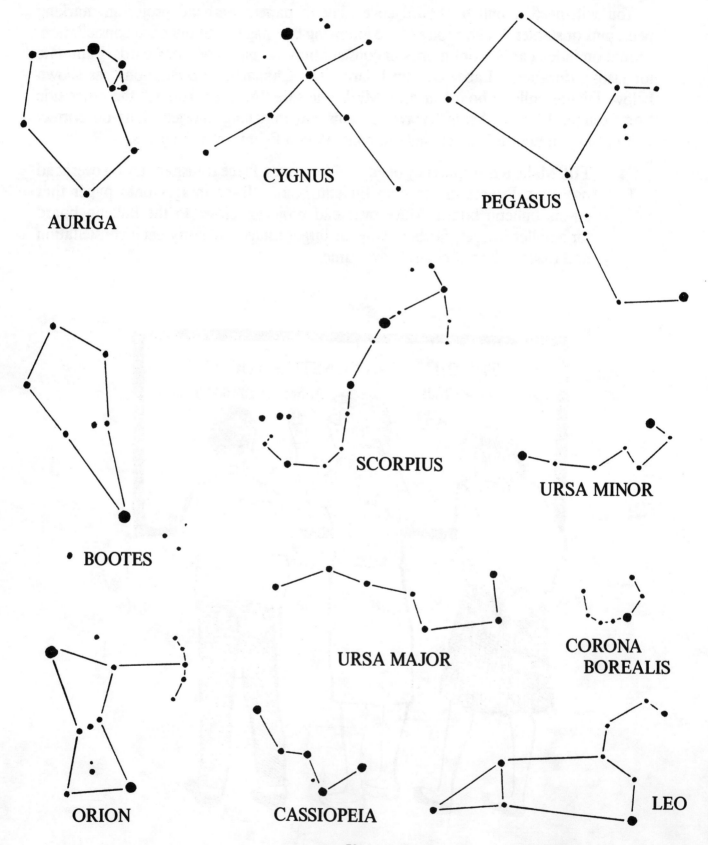

AURIGA

CYGNUS

PEGASUS

BOOTES

SCORPIUS

URSA MINOR

URSA MAJOR

CORONA BOREALIS

ORION

CASSIOPEIA

LEO

THE CHANGING CONSTELLATIONS

AS SEEN IN 100,000 YEARS

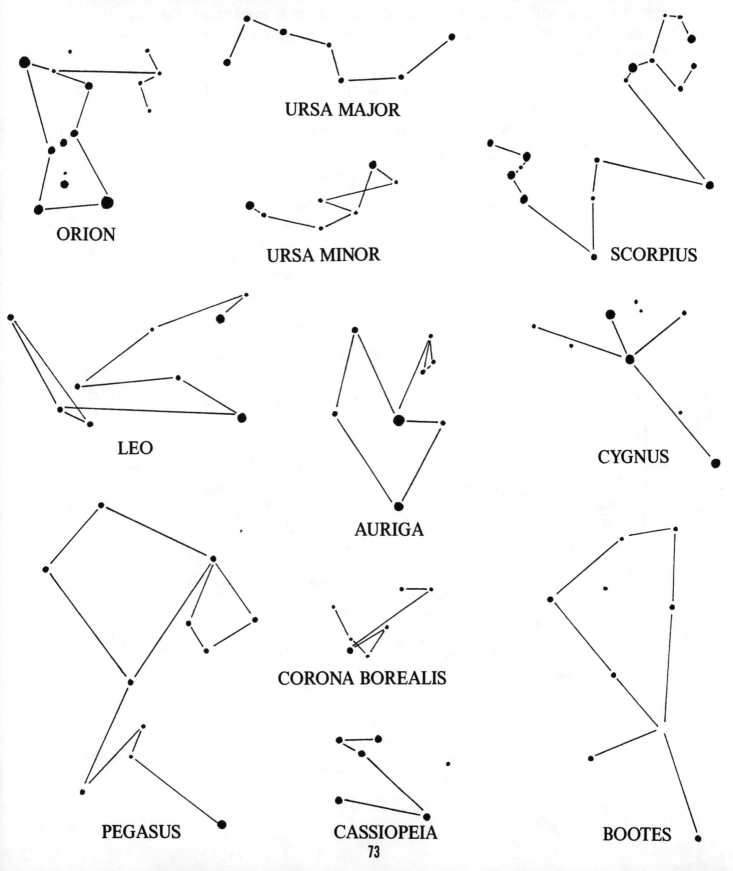

ORION

URSA MAJOR

URSA MINOR

SCORPIUS

LEO

AURIGA

CYGNUS

PEGASUS

CORONA BOREALIS

CASSIOPEIA

BOOTES

PIZZA WHEEL SKY CHART THAT SHOWS CONSTELLATION BOUNDARIES

You will need a pizza wheel or other stiff cardboard, scissors and glue. Make a copy of this page. Have students cut out the sky chart below. Tape or glue to pizza wheel or other stiff cardboard. Students then drop a marker on the sky. Identify the constellation by its scientific name and by its common name, for example, Ursa Major, the Big Bear.

 TIP: Disc can be made into a spinner game or mounted on a thick sheet of cardboard and used as a dart game. In any event, students should become familiar with both the scientific and common names for each constellation on the disc.

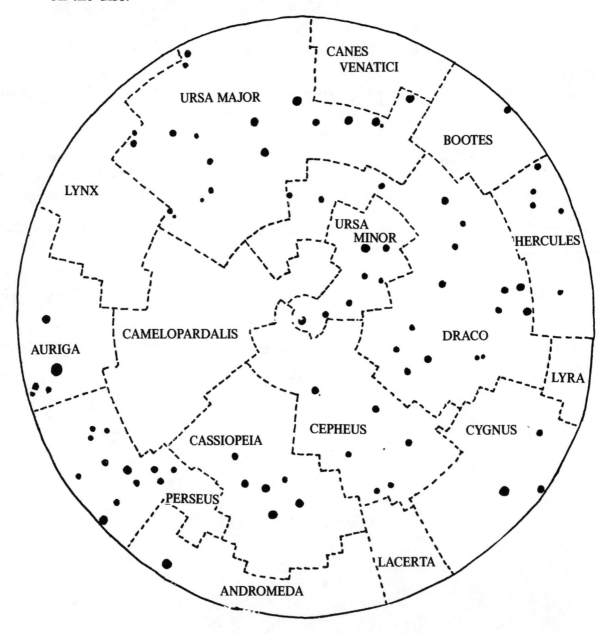

THE ECLIPTIC

Each star on each copymaster is plotted with the aid of a grid near its exact celestial coordinates which include a star's *right ascension (R.A.)* and *declination (Dec.)*. The declination of a star, expressed in units of degrees, minutes and seconds, is measured either north (+) or south (–) of the imaginary line in the sky called the *celestial equator*. A corresponding terrestrial measurement would be that of *latitude*. The *right ascension* of a star, which is equivalent to *longitude* on earth, is measured eastward from a point in the sky called the vernal (spring) equinox (see page 76).

In its yearly journey around the sky, the sun crosses the celestial equator at two points, once when it crosses going south and once when it crosses going north (see Figure 5). The point of intersection between the ecliptic and the celestial equator where the sun travels north is called the vernal equinox. The other crossing point is called the autumnal equinox. These two points mark the position of the sun in the sky on the first day of spring, March 21, and on the first day of autumn, September 21, respectively. The right ascension of a star is measured eastward from the vernal equinox in units of hours from 0 to 24. The hour lines, as they are called, are spaced 15° apart along the celestial equator and converge like the spokes of a wheel going towards the hub at the north and south celestial poles. If one observes the lines of longitude on the earth, you will see the same phenomenon. The hours of right ascension are divided further into sixty minutes and each minute is divided into sixty seconds.

Figure 5 shows the positions of the vernal and autumnal equinox and the major divisions of right ascension and declination. The position of the sun on June 21, the summer solstice, and on December 21, the winter solstice, are also shown. These dates mark the beginning of summer and winter respectively in the Northern Hemisphere.

Once celestial coordinates of the stars are identified, it is easy to plot their correct positions with respect to one another and obtain the familiar pattern of the constellations in the sky.

THE ECLIPTIC

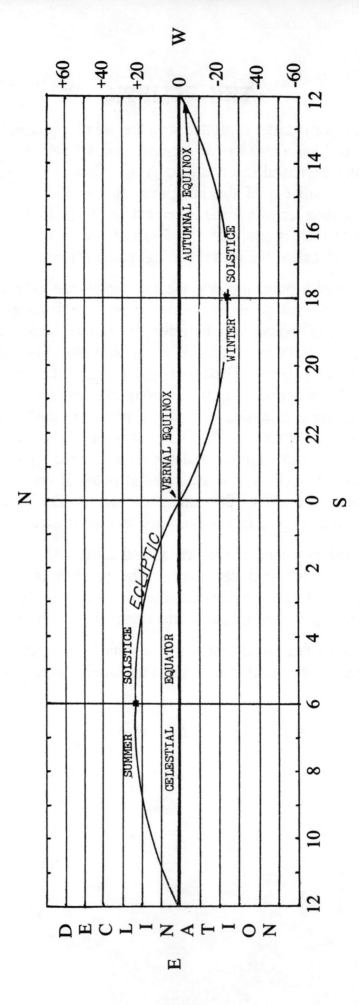

RIGHT ASCENSION

Figure 5

76

FOLD-OUT WALL SKY CHART OF CONSTELLATION BOUNDARIES

You will need a copy of each of the following four pages, tape or glue, laminating machine, magnetic tape if available, and scissors. Make copies of each of the four pages. Tape pages together at tab marks. Laminate. Place thin strip of magnetic tape on *ecliptic*. Cut out astronaut below. Laminate. Mount magnetic tape to back of astronaut. Attach to magnetic ecliptic line. Post for all to see. Each day move astronaut along ecliptic from one constellation to the next, starting with Virgo, the first day of fall, and moving on to Leo, the last day of summer. Have students draw and study each day's constellation. Classify the constellations according to the season during which they can be seen.

 TIP: Teach students that the *ecliptic* is the apparent path the sun and the planets follow when traveling around the sky. Teach students that the dotted lines on the chart represent rather arbitrary boundaries between constellations. Similar to lines that mark boundaries between various towns, cities, states and countries, these lines are invisible and represent a general dividing line between constellations.

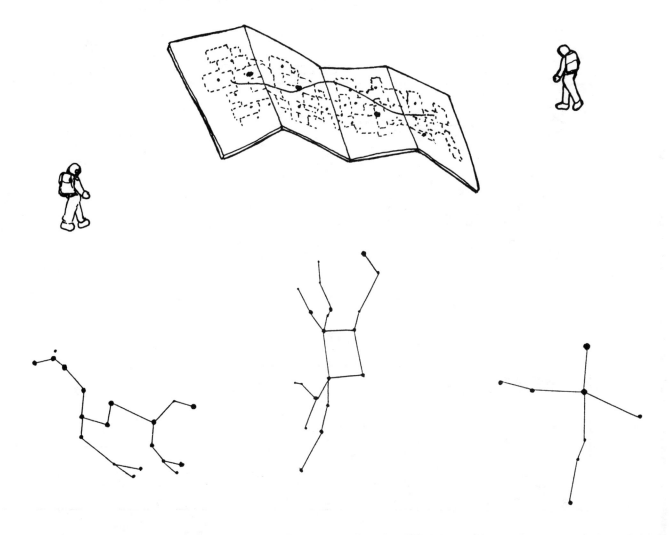

77

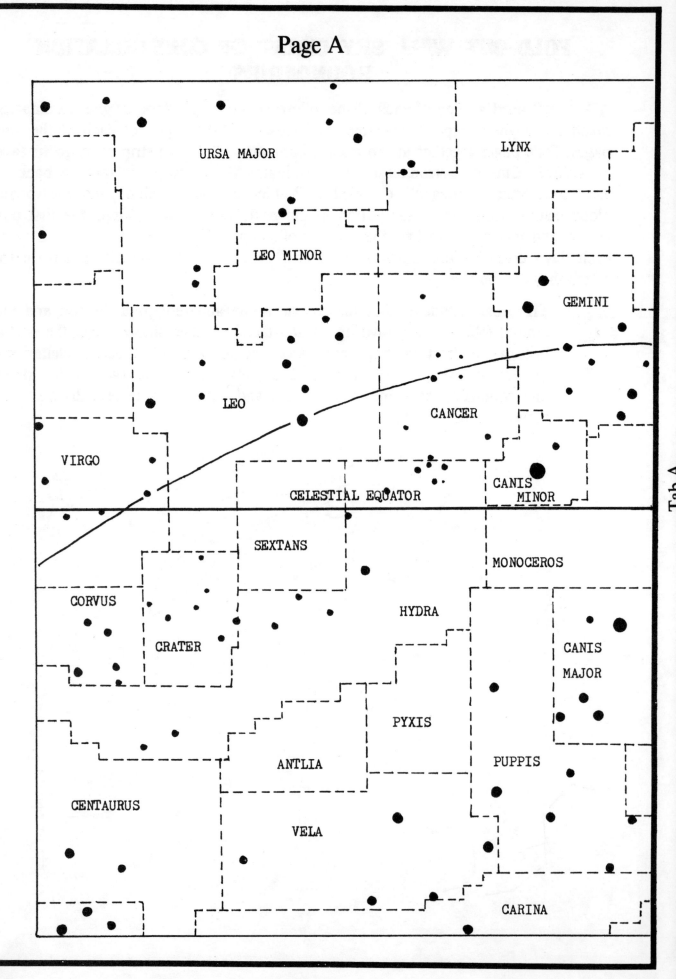

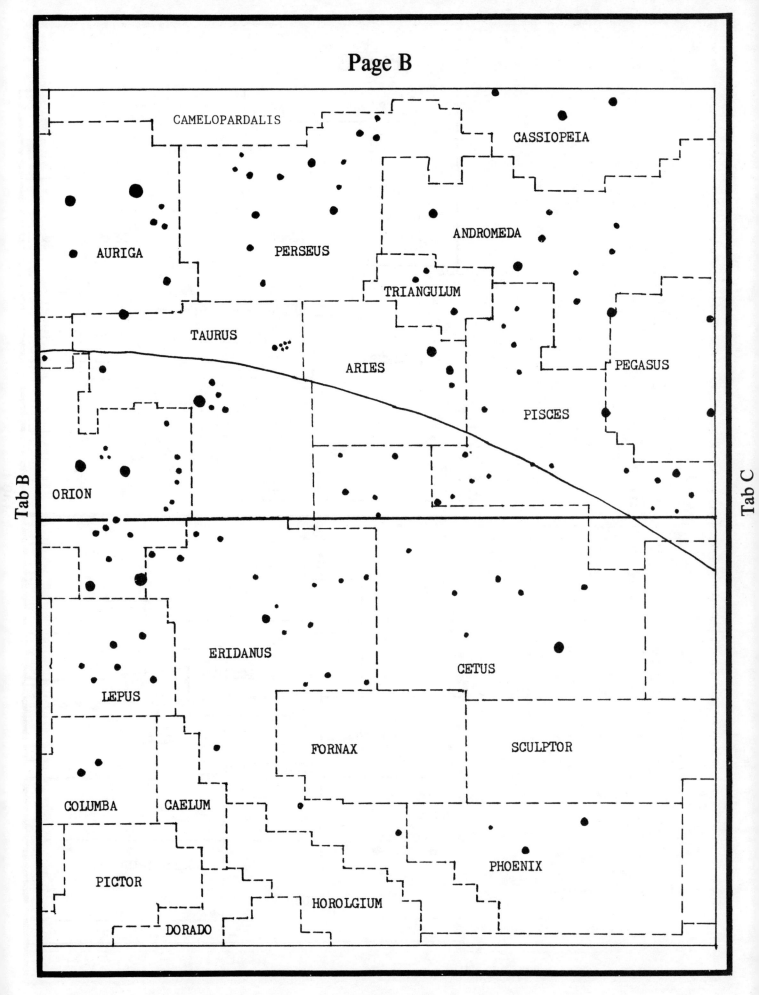

Tab B

Tab C

CAMELOPARDALIS

CASSIOPEIA

ANDROMEDA

AURIGA

PERSEUS

TRIANGULUM

TAURUS

ARIES

PEGASUS

PISCES

ORION

ERIDANUS

CETUS

LEPUS

FORNAX

SCULPTOR

COLUMBA   CAELUM

PICTOR

PHOENIX

HOROLGIUM

DORADO

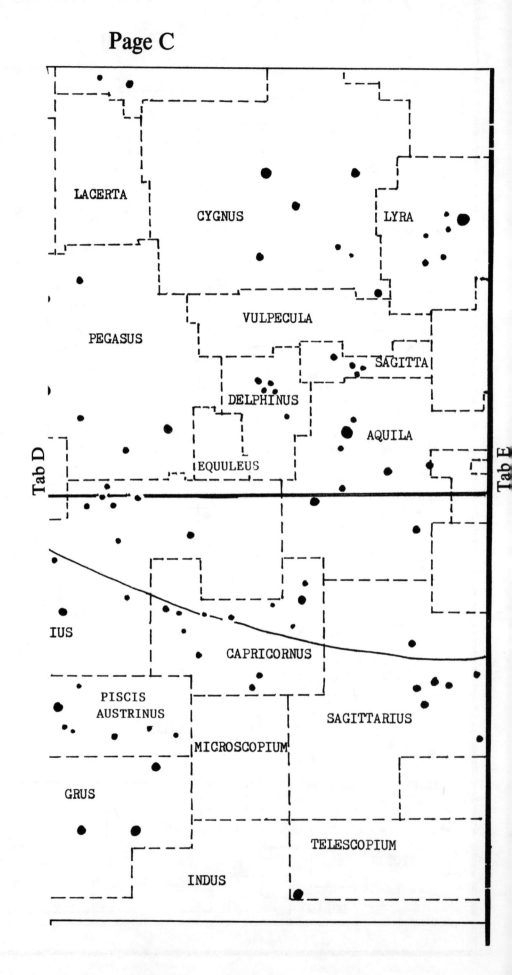

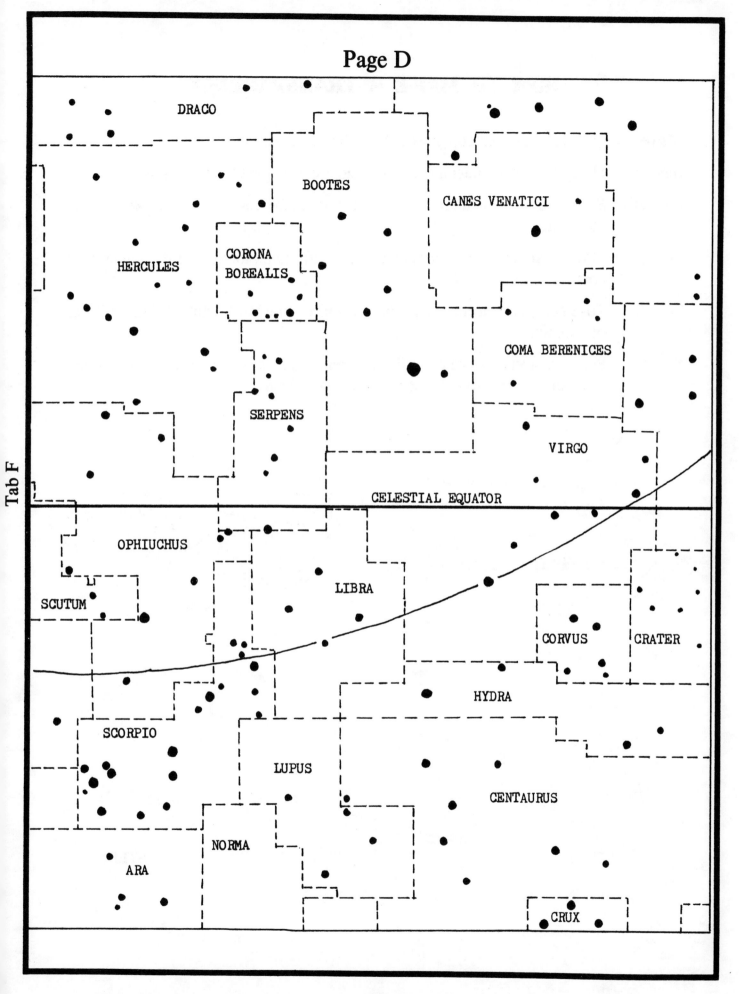

Tab F

DRACO

BOOTES

CANES VENATICI

HERCULES

CORONA
BOREALIS

COMA BERENICES

SERPENS

VIRGO

CELESTIAL EQUATOR

OPHIUCHUS

LIBRA

SCUTUM

CORVUS | CRATER

HYDRA

SCORPIO

LUPUS

CENTAURUS

NORMA

ARA

CRUX

HOW TO MAKE A TRANSPARENCY

Make transparencies of each copymaster by following these steps:

Step 1: Using a copying machine, make a clear copy of each desired page.

Step 2: Set the dial on a thermofax copying machine towards the darker end of the scale.

Step 3: Place heat sensitive acetate over copy with notch located in the upper right corner.

Step 4: Together, place acetate and copy in top of machine. Remove from bottom of machine.

Step 5: Separate acetate from copy. Transparency is now made. You are now ready to mount the transparency on a cardboard frame.

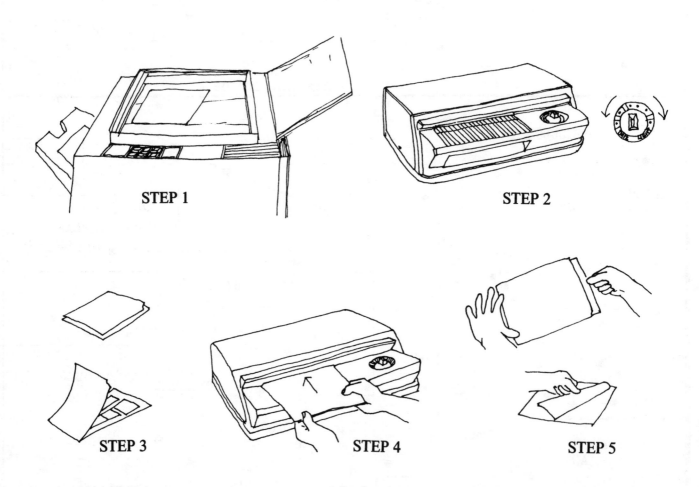

STEP 1

STEP 2

STEP 3

STEP 4

STEP 5

THIRTY-FIVE COMPLETE MATCHING CONSTELLATION COPYMASTERS

Here is a set of thirty-five constellation copymasters. Make copies of each copymaster for each of your students. The copymasters contain extending information that features the location of interesting objects that can be seen with the aid of a small telescope or in some cases, a pair of binoculars. These special objects are given numbers, found on each copymaster page. These objects were catalogued by Charles Messier, an eighteenth century French astronomer. Thus, on the copymasters one finds objects labelled M35, M42 and M1. Messier's catalog, found in an astronomy book, can then be used to learn what these numbers actually mean. For example, M35 means an open cluster in Gemini, M42 means the Orion Nebula and M1 means the Crab Nebula in Taurus. The chart below contains a portion of Messier's catalog.

TIP: Copymasters may be used for large group, small group or individualized instruction. As each copymaster is introduced, students will quickly discover interesting information about each constellation. A booklet of thirty-five copymasters that represents over forty-three constellations in this book can be given to each student for a lifetime of enjoyment.

M	R.A.		DEC.		MAG.	DESCRIPTION
	h	m	°			
M 1	5	33	22	0	8.4	Crab Nebulae in Taurus
M 2	21	32	-0	56	6.3	Globular Cluster in Aquarius
M 3	13	41.1	28	30	6.4	Globular Cluster in Canes Venatici
M 4	16	22.1	-26	27	6.4	Globular Cluster in Scorpio
M 5	15	17.3	2	11	6.2	Globular Cluster in Serpens
M 6	17	38.4	-32	12	4.5	Open Cluster in Scorpio
M 7	17	52.3	-34	48	3.5	Open Cluster in Scorpio
M 8	18	1.6	-24	23	5.0	"Lagoon" Nebulae in Sagittarius
M 9	17	17.7	-18	30	8.0	Globular Cluster in Ophiuchus
M 10	16	55.8	-4	04	6.7	Globular Cluster in Ophiuchus
M 11	18	49.7	-6	18	6.3	Open Cluster in Scutum
M 12	16	45.9	-1	55	6.6	Globular Cluster in Ophiuchus
M 13	16	40.8	36	30	5.7	Globular Cluster in Hercules
M 14	17	36.3	-3	16	6.0	Globular Cluster in Ophiuchus

Copymaster 1: Andromeda

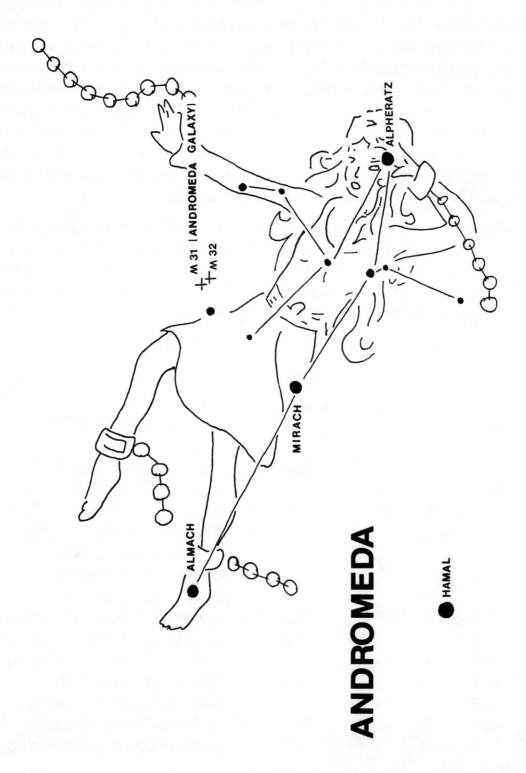

ANDROMEDA

AQUARIUS

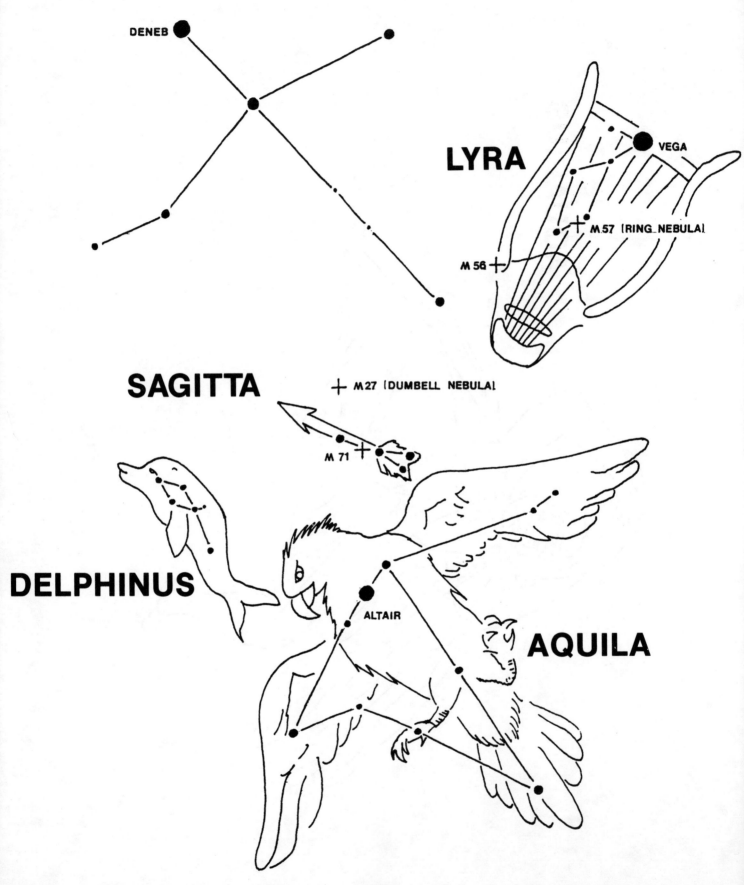

DENEB

LYRA

VEGA

M 57 (RING NEBULA)

M 56

SAGITTA

+ M 27 (DUMBELL NEBULA)

M 71

DELPHINUS

ALTAIR

AQUILA

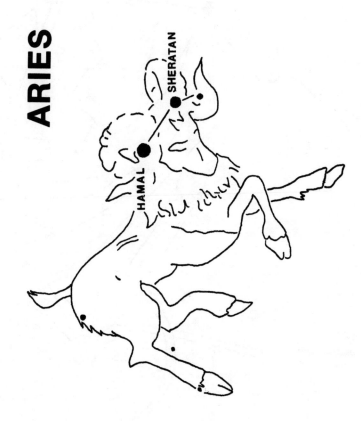

AURIGA

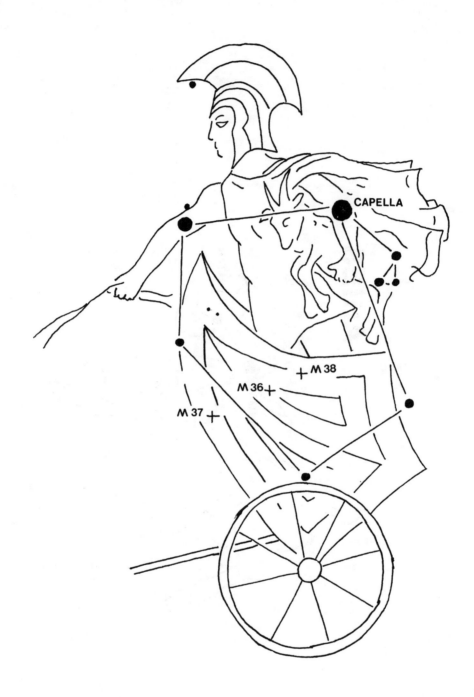

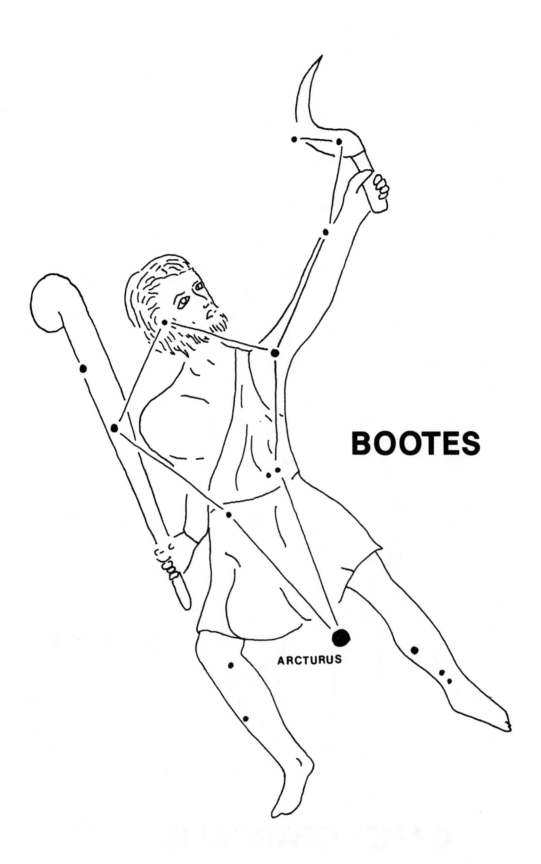

BOOTES

ARCTURUS

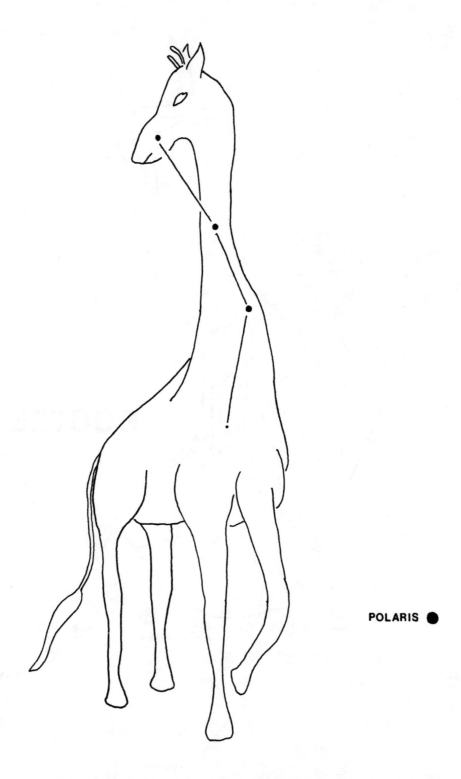

POLARIS ●

CAMELOPARDALIS

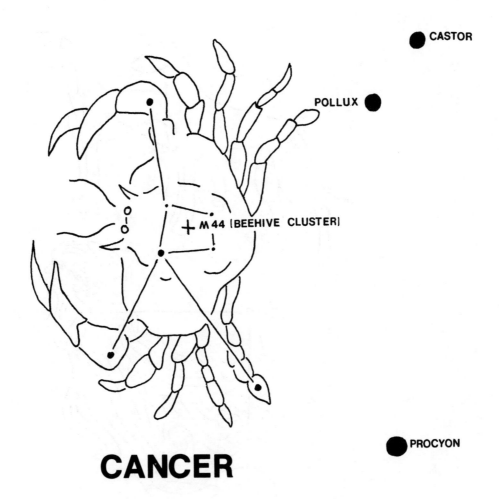

CASTOR

POLLUX

+ M 44 [BEEHIVE CLUSTER]

PROCYON

CANCER

CANES VENATICI

COMA BERENICES

●ARCTURUS

CANIS MINOR

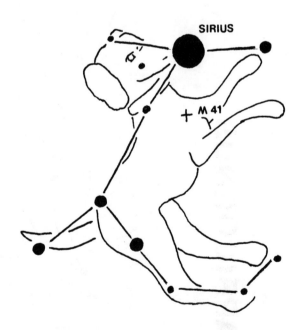

CANIS MAJOR

ALTAIR

CAPRICORNUS

M 30

CASSIOPEIA

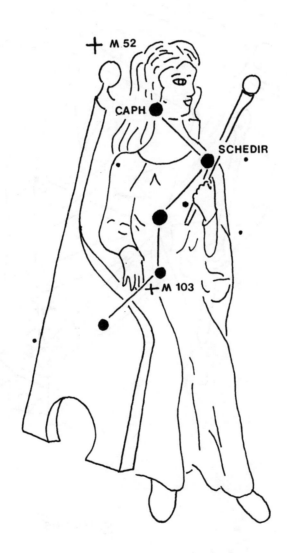

CEPHEUS

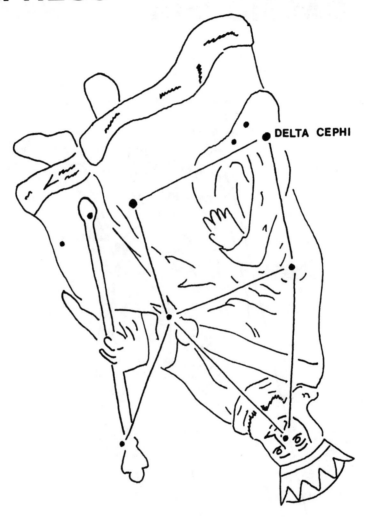

DELTA CEPHI

POLARIS

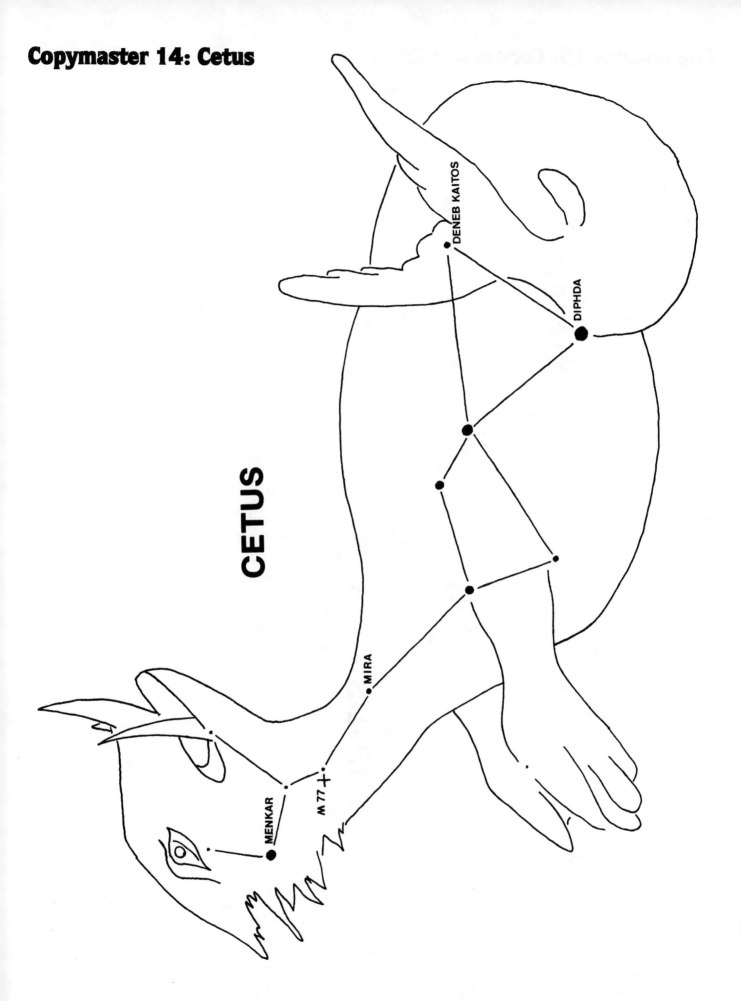

CETUS

DENEB KAITOS

DIPHDA

MIRA

MENKAR

M 77

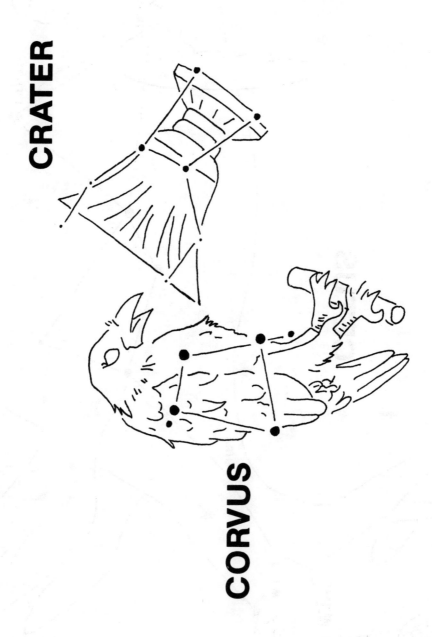

CRATER

CORVUS

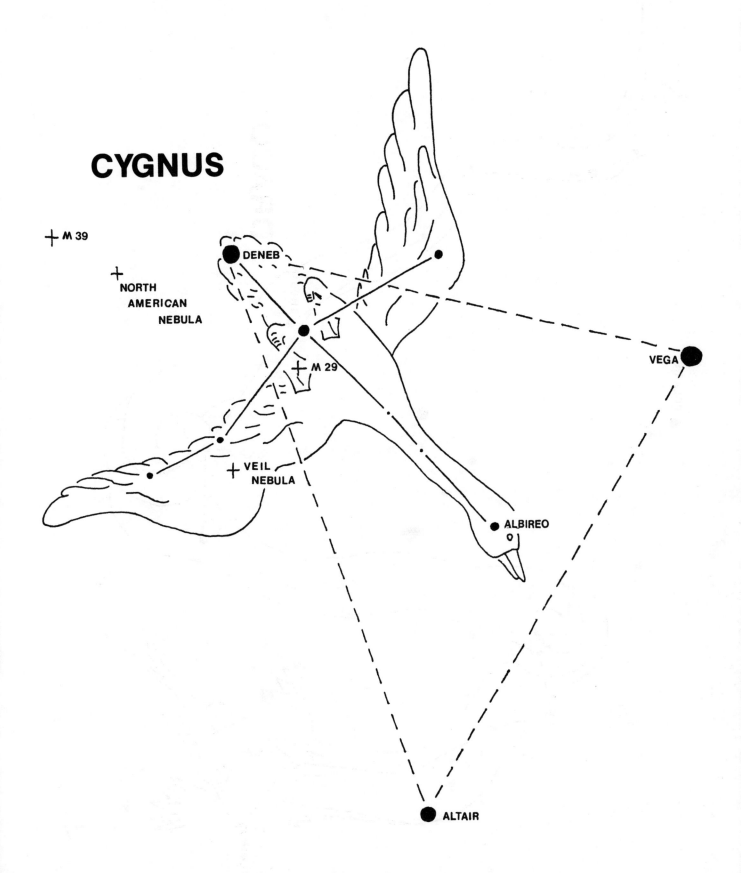

CYGNUS

M 39

NORTH
AMERICAN
NEBULA

DENEB

M 29

VEIL
NEBULA

ALBIREO

VEGA

ALTAIR

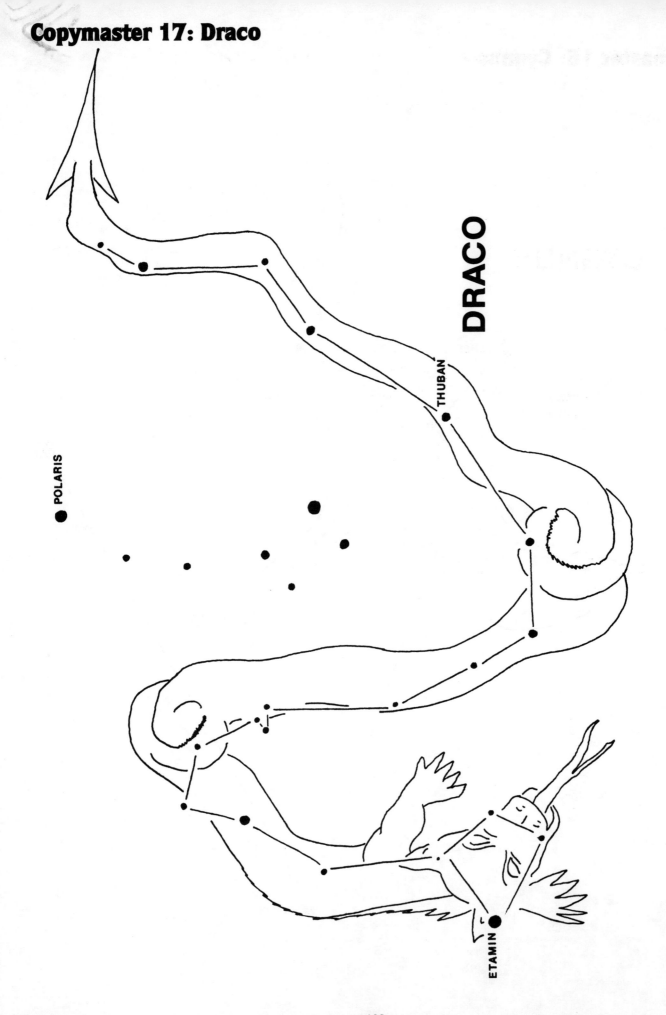

DRACO

POLARIS

THUBAN

ETAMIN

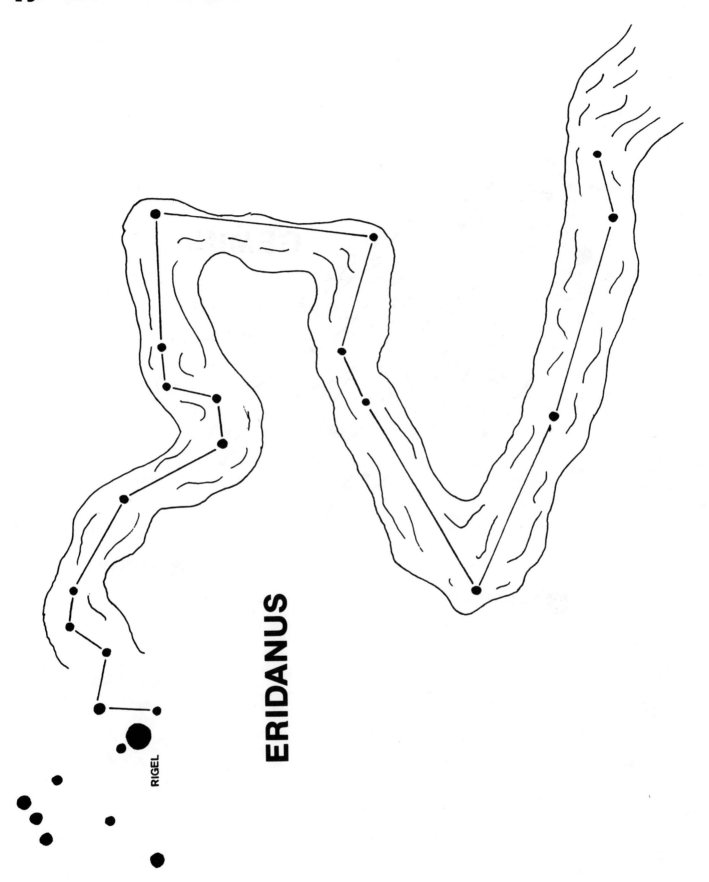

ERIDANUS

RIGEL

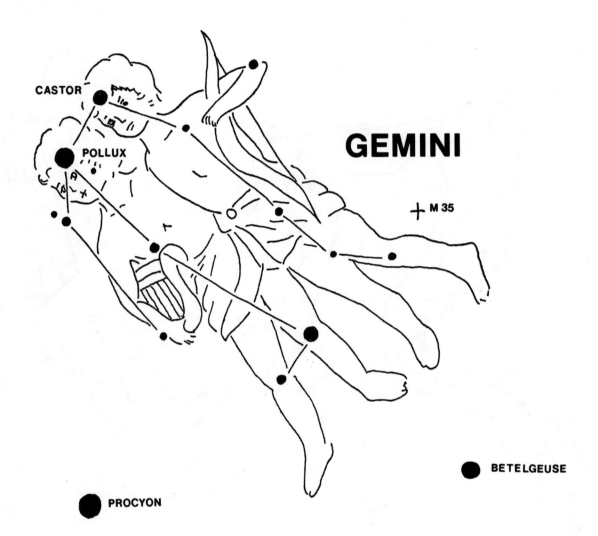

GEMINI

CASTOR

POLLUX

+ M 35

BETELGEUSE

PROCYON

SIRIUS

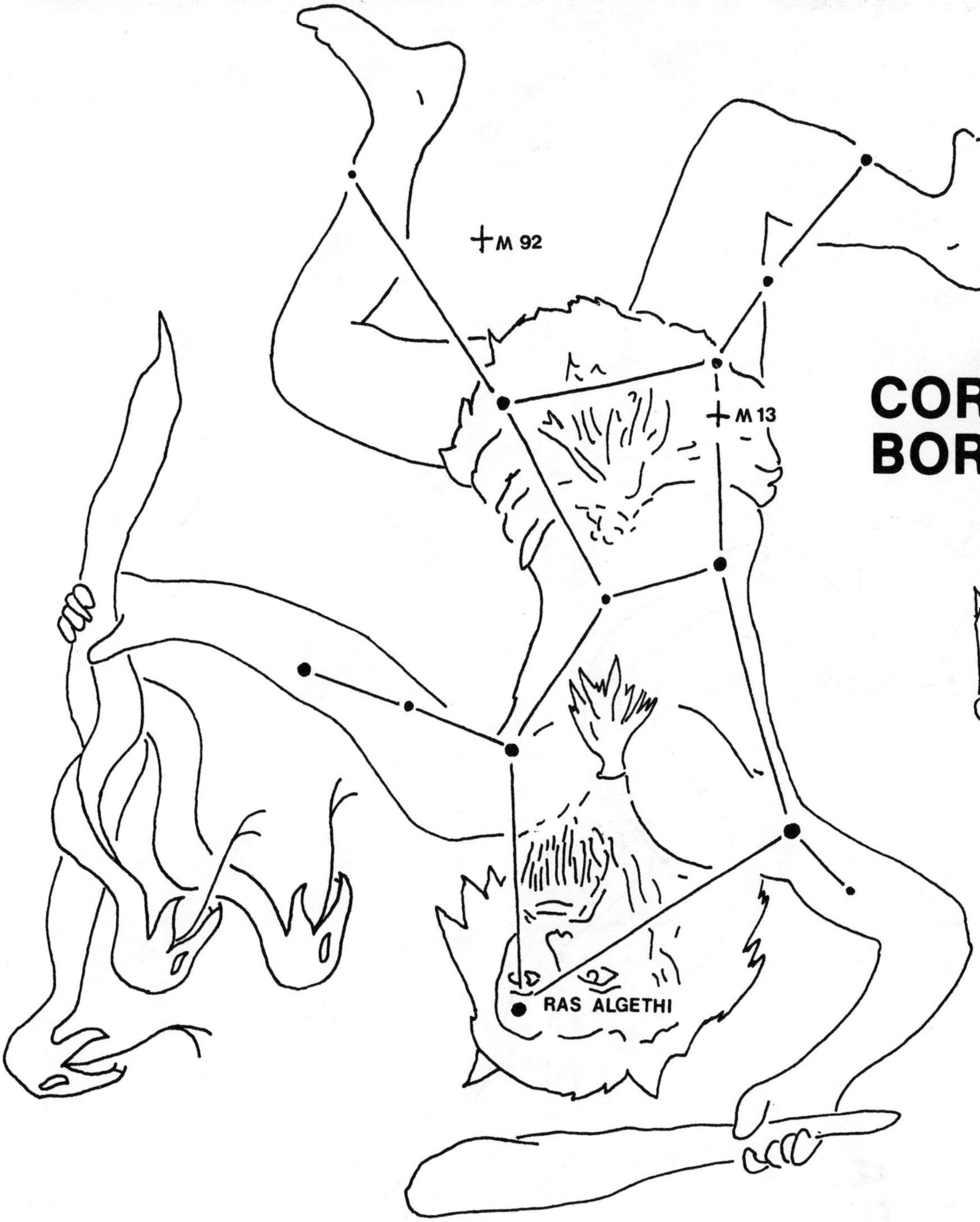

+M 92

CORONA BOREALIS

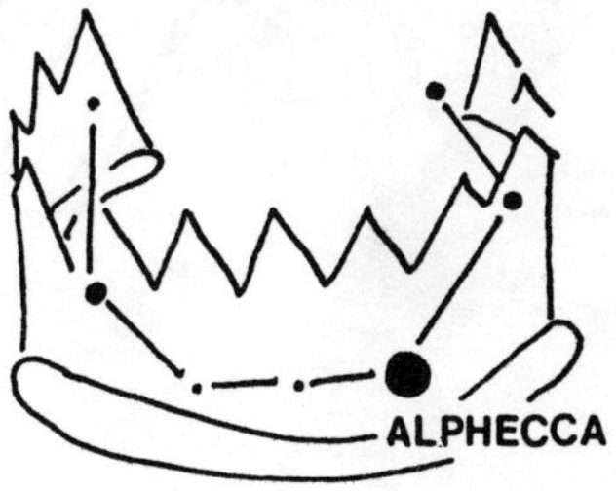

+M 13

ALPHECCA

RAS ALGETHI

HERCULES

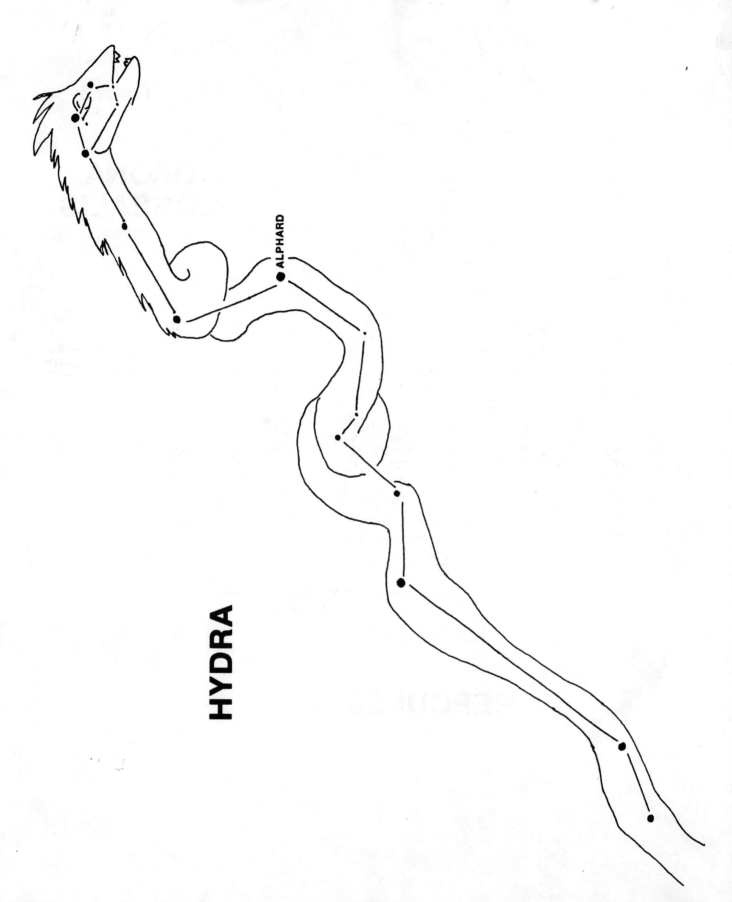

ALPHARD

HYDRA

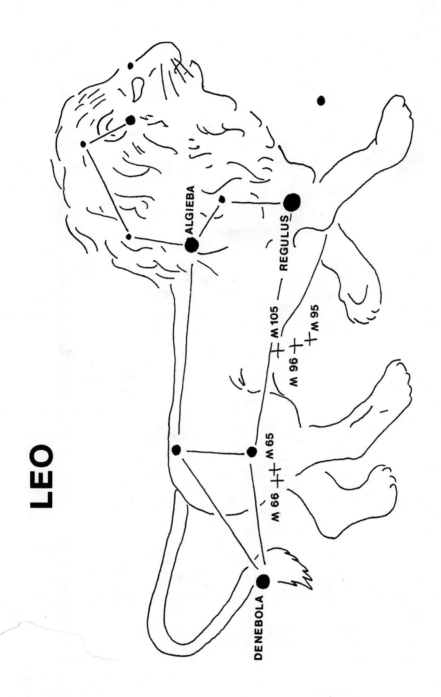

LEO

ALGIEBA

REGULUS

DENEBOLA

M 105

M 96

M 95

M 65

M 66

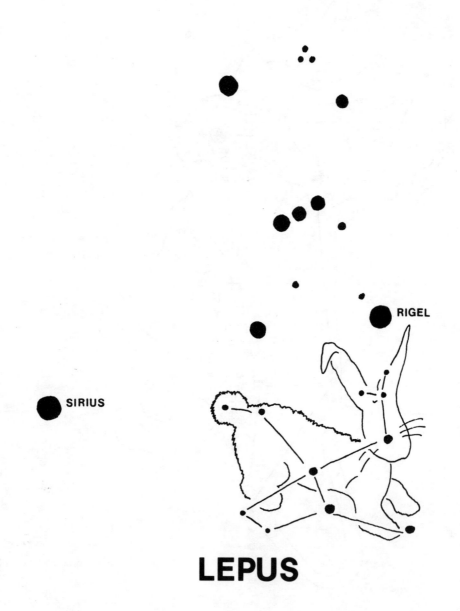

LEPUS

Copymaster 24: Libra and Scorpius

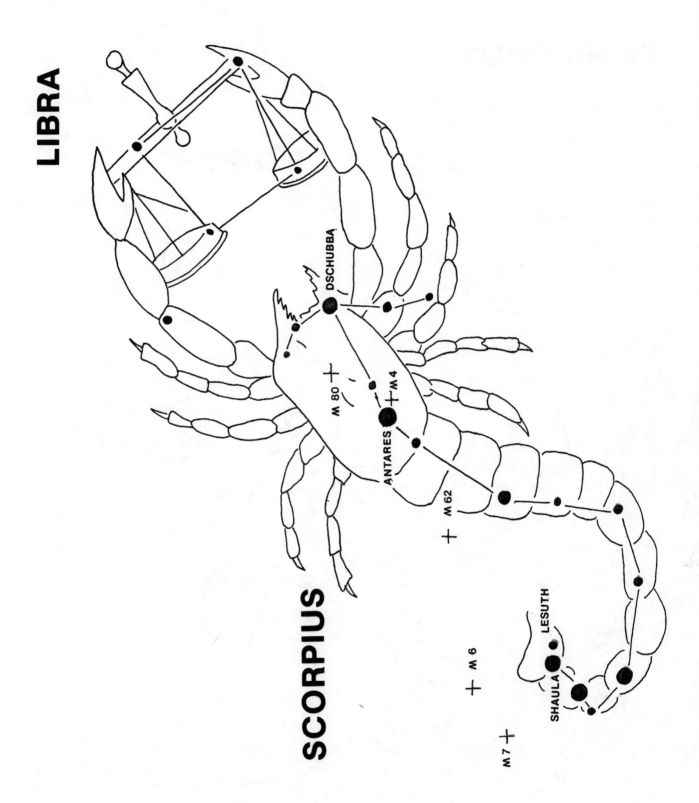

LIBRA

SCORPIUS

DSCHUBBA

M 80

M 4

ANTARES

M 62

LESUTH

M 6

SHAULA

M 7

OPHIUCHUS

SERPENS

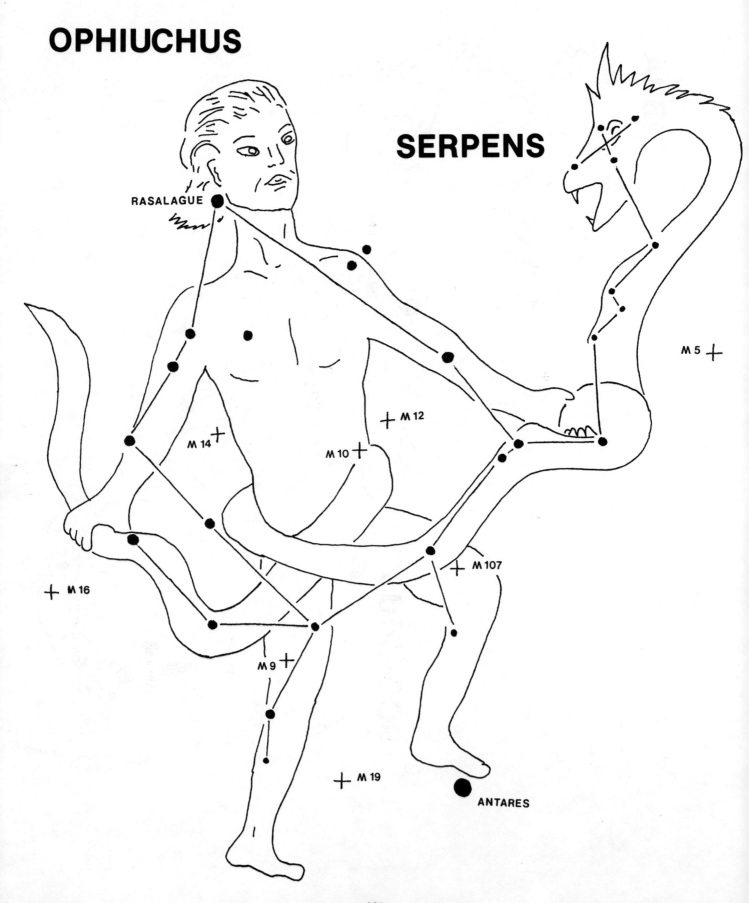

RASALAGUE

M 5 +

M 12 +

M 14 +

M 10 +

M 107 +

+ M 16

M 9 +

+ M 19

ANTARES

ORION

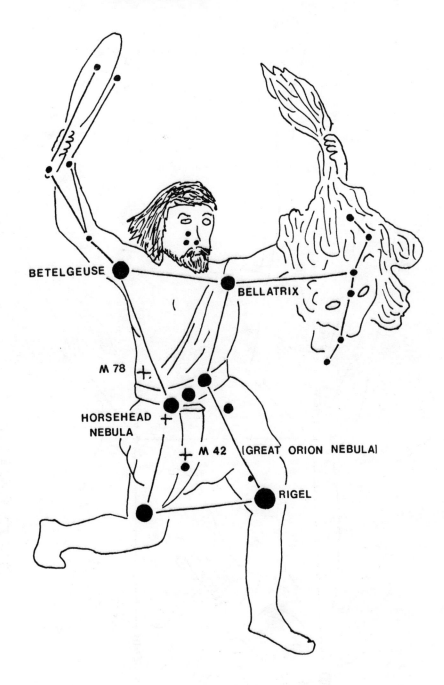

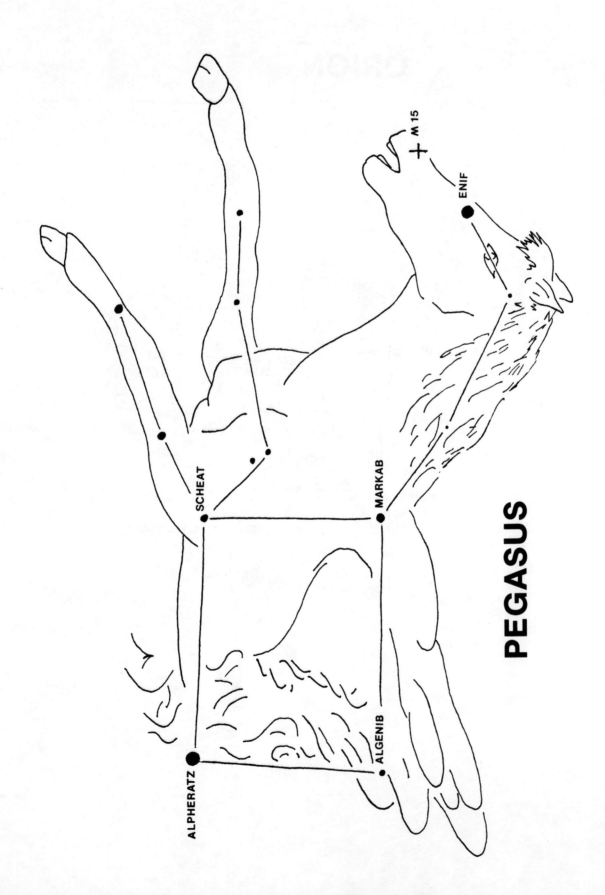

PEGASUS

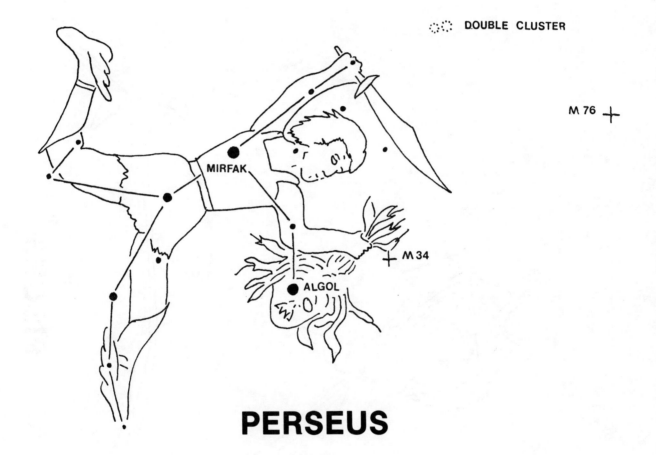

DOUBLE CLUSTER

M 76

MIRFAK

M 34

ALGOL

PERSEUS

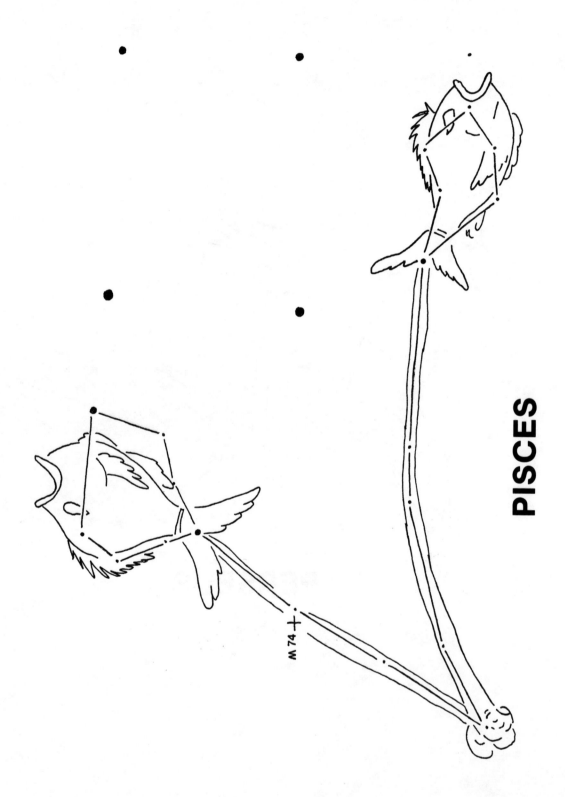

PISCES

M 74

PISCIS AUSTRINUS

FOMALHAUT

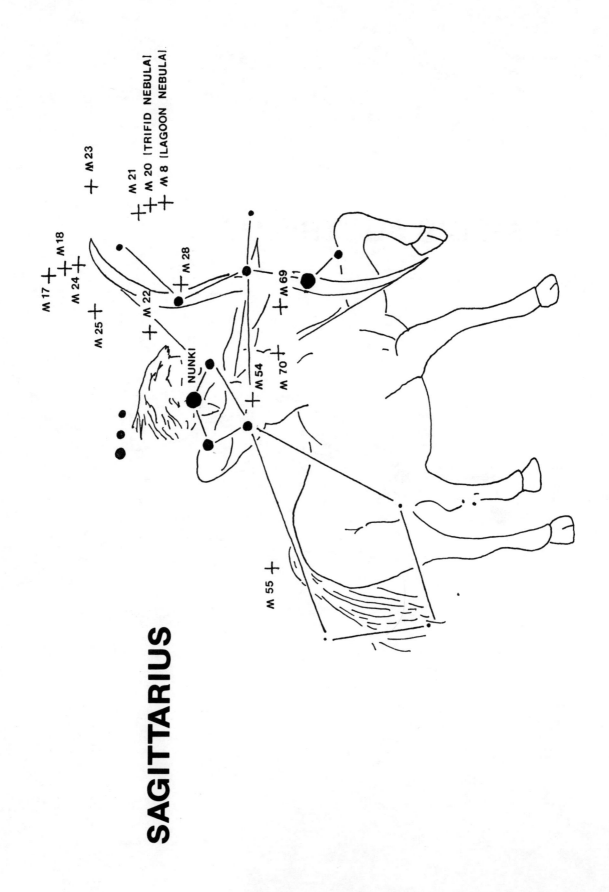

SAGITTARIUS

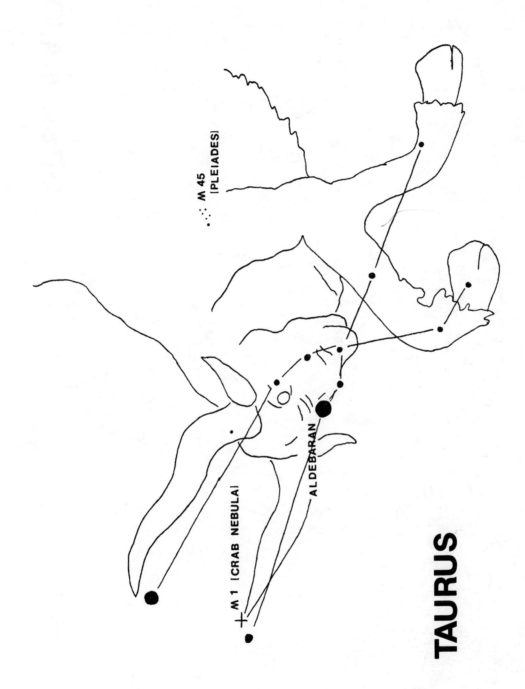

M 45
(PLEIADES)

M 1 (CRAB NEBULA)

ALDEBARAN

TAURUS

Copymaster 33: Ursa Major

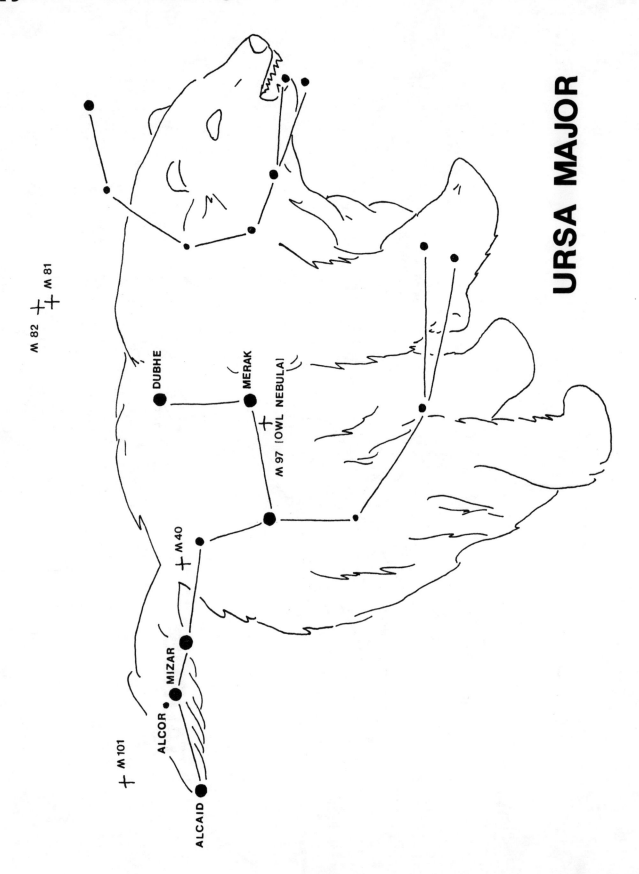

URSA MAJOR

M 82 + M 81

DUBHE

MERAK

M 97 (OWL NEBULA)

M 40

ALCOR • MIZAR

M 101

ALCAID

URSA MINOR

POLARIS

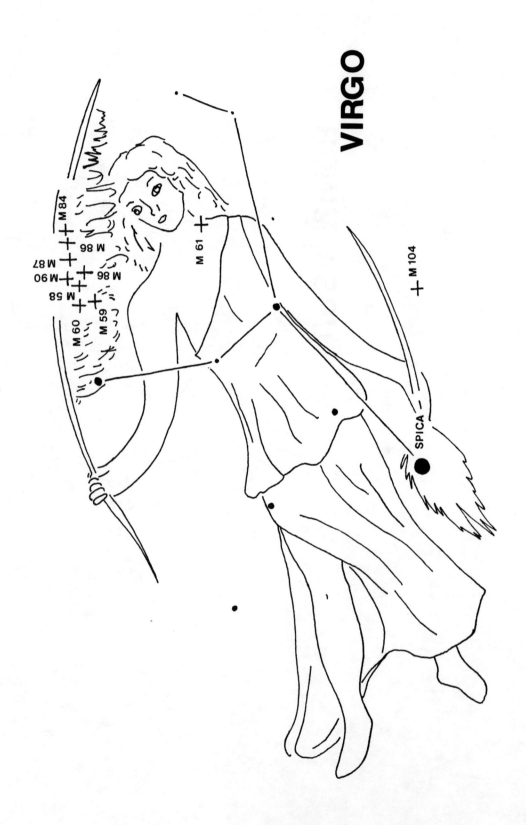

VIRGO

M 84

M 98

M 86

M 87

M 90

M 58

M 60

M 59

M 61

M 104

SPICA

ASTRONOMY PUZZLES

CONSTELLATIONS

THE STARS 1

THE SPRING SKY

THE WINTER SKY

THE FALL SKY

THE SUMMER SKY

ANSWERS TO PUZZLES

CONSTELLATIONS

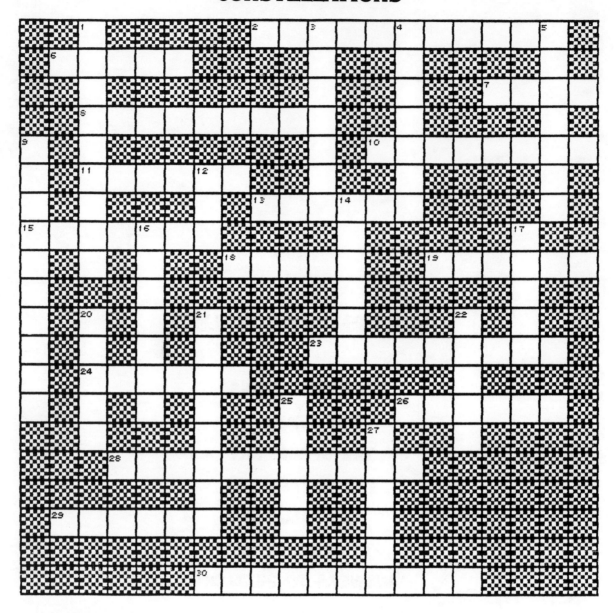

ACROSS CLUES

2. The Sea Goat
6. Zodiac constellation that follows Pisces
7. Part of the Summer Triangle contains the star Vega
8. Daughter of Cassiopeia and Cepheus
10. Hero found between the Harp and the Northern Crown
11. Southern most constellation of the Summer Triangle
13. Constellation in which the sun can be found on March 21
15. Contains the giant star Antares
18. The Great Hunter of the Winter Sky
19. The Twins of the Winter Sky
23. "Little Bear"
24. Aldebaran and the Seven Sisters can be found here
26. The Crow
28. The Archer _____ follows the Scorpion
29. Arcturus can be found at the bottom of the Kite
30. Big Dog

DOWN CLUES

1. "Big Bear"
3. The Great Square of _____
4. The King of the sky
5. In the grasp of Ophiuchus
9. The "W"
12. Regulus is the brightest star in this constellation
14. The Crab
16. The hero who saved Andromeda from the Whale Monster
17. The blue-white star Spica is found here
20. The Whale Monster
21. The Water Carrier
22. In the grasp of the Scorpion
25. Found weaving its tail between Ursa Major and Ursa Minor
27. Pentagon

120

CONSTELLATIONS

ACROSS

2

6

7

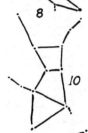

8

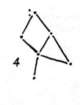

10

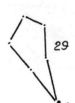

11

13

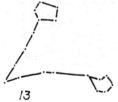

15

18

19

23

24

26

28

29

30

DOWN

1

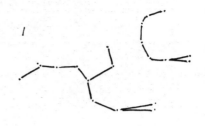

17

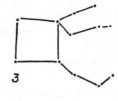

3

20

4

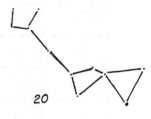

21

22

5

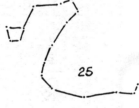

25

9

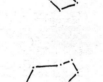

27

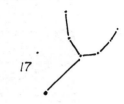

12

14

16

THE STARS 1

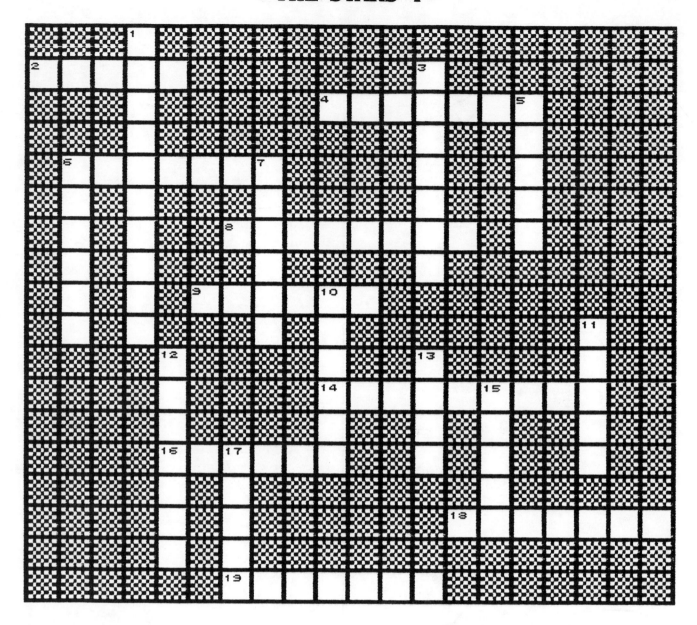

ACROSS CLUES

2. The knee of Orion
4. The brightest star in the constellation of Aurgia
6. The North Star
8. The tail of the Kite
9. Belongs to the tail of the Dragon; once was the Pole Star
14. The eye of the Bull
16. One of the Twins
18. The head of the Swan
19. The heart of the Scorpion

DOWN CLUES

1. Found in the shoulder of the Great Hunter
3. The heart of the Lion
5. The eclipsing variable star of Perseus
6. The other Twin
7. The brightest star in the sky as viewed from the earth
10. The head of the Eagle
11. The tail of the Swan
12. Star belonging to the Little Dog
13. Brightest star of the Summer Triangle
15. The eye of Medusa
17. The arc to Arcturus: Spike to _____

THE STARS 1

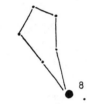

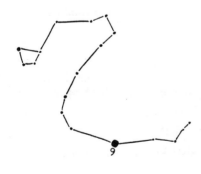

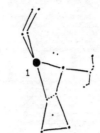

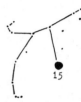

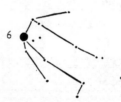

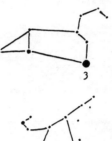

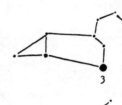

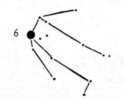

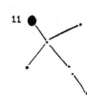

THE SPRING SKY

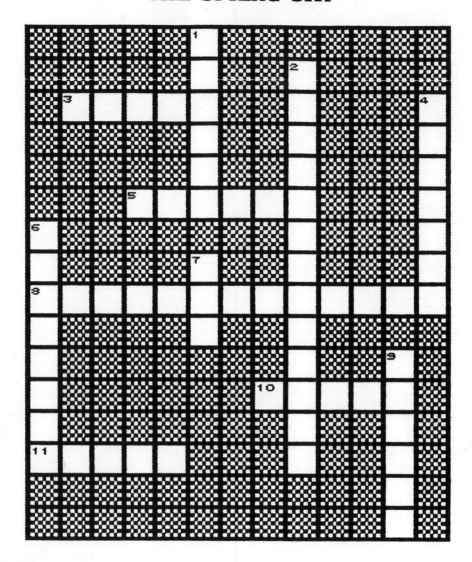

ACROSS CLUES
3. The Sea Serpent
5. The Crow
8. The hair of Bernices
10. The Virgin
11. Alpha Virginis

DOWN CLUES
1. The Cup
2. The Hunting Dogs of the Herdsman
4. The heart of the Lion
6. The tail of the Kite
7. The king of Beasts
9. The Kite

THE WINTER SKY

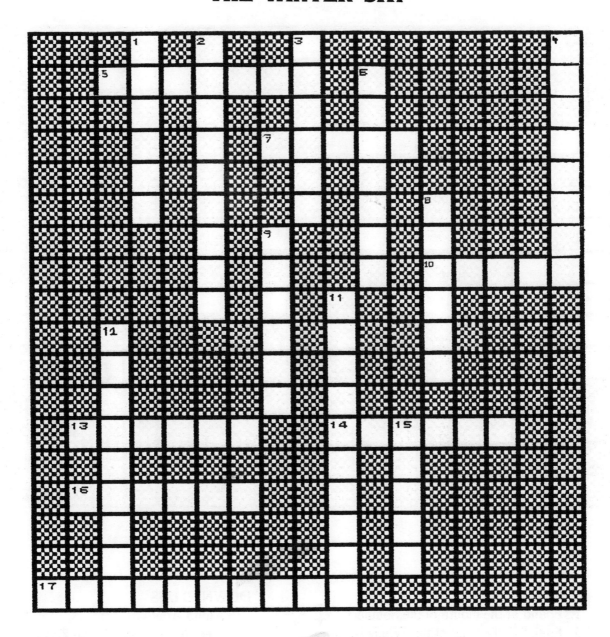

ACROSS CLUES

5. Found at a corner of a Pentagon
7. The Great Hunter
10. The Rabbit
13. The Twins
14. The brightest star seen from Earth (the Dog Star)
16. The Crab
17. The Big Dog

DOWN CLUES

1. One of the Twins
2. The bright red star in the shoulder of the Great Hunter
3. The Bull
4. The winding river of the sky
6. The Little Dog Star
8. The other Twin
9. The Pentagon
11. The Little Dog
12. The eye of the Bull
15. The knee of Orion

THE FALL SKY

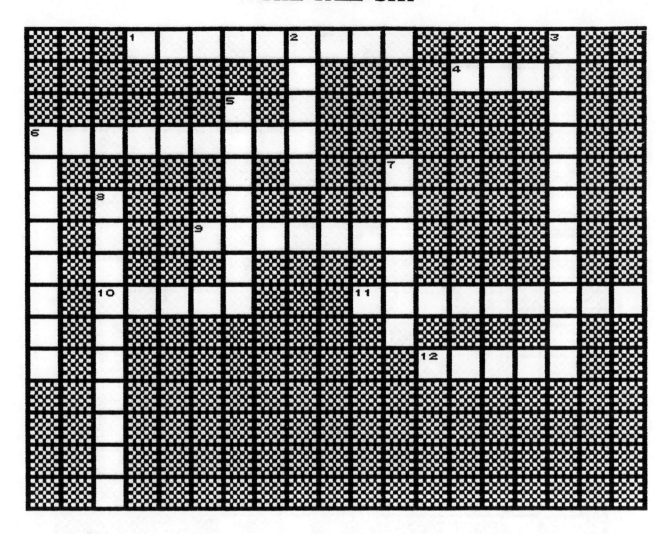

ACROSS CLUES
1. Found at the mouth of the Southern Fish
4. Found at the neck of the Whale Monster
6. The daughter of Cepheus
9. The Winged Pony
10. The Ram
11. Found between Aquila and Pegasus
12. The Whale Monster

DOWN CLUES
2. Alpha Arietis
3. Precedes Aquarius in the Zodiac
5. Carries the head of Medusa
6. Water Carrier
7. Two Fish
8. The Triangle

THE SUMMER SKY

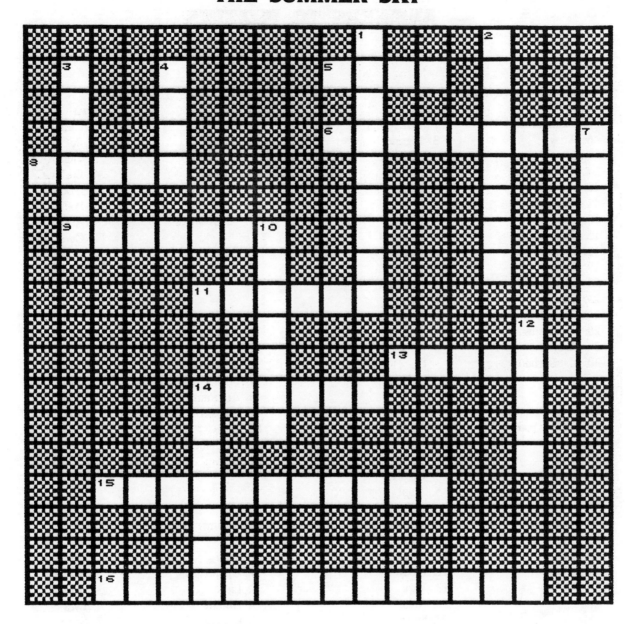

ACROSS CLUES
5. The brightest star in the Summer Triangle
6. The Serpent Holder
8. The Scales
9. The heart of the Scorpion
11. The Swan
13. In the grasps of Ophiuchus
14. The southernmost star of the Summer Triangle
15. The Archer
16. The Northern Crown

DOWN CLUES
1. The Dolphin
2. The son of Zeus
3. The Eagle
4. The Harp
7. The holder of the Scales
10. The arrow shot by Hercules
12. The tail of the Swan
14. Double star found at the head of the Swan

ANSWERS TO PUZZLES

Constellations, page 120

Across
2. Capricornus
6. Aries
7. Lyra
8. Andromeda
10. Hercules
11. Aquila
13. Pisces
15. Scorpio
18. Orion
19. Gemini
23. Ursa Minor
24. Taurus
26. Corvus
28. Sagittarius
29. Bootes
30. Canis Major

Down
1. Ursa Major
3. Pegasus
4. Cepheus
5. Serpens
9. Cassiopeia
12. Leo
14. Cancer
16. Perseus
17. Virgo
20. Cetus
21. Aquarius
22. Libra
25. Draco
27. Auriga

The Stars 1, page 122

Across
2. Rigel
4. Capella
6. Polaris
8. Arcturus
9. Thuban
14. Aldebaran
16. Castor
18. Albireo
19. Antares

Down
1. Betelgeuse
3. Regulus
5. Algol
6. Pollux
7. Sirius
10. Altair
11. Deneb
12. Procyon
13. Vega
15. Algol
17. Spica

The Spring Sky, page 124

Across
3. Hydra
5. Corvus
8. Coma Berenices
10. Virgo
11. Spica

Down
1. Crater
2. Canes Venatici
4. Regulus
6. Arcturus
7. Leo
9. Bootes

The Winter Sky, page 125

Across
5. Capella
7. Orion
10. Lepus
13. Gemini
14. Sirius
16. Cancer
17. Canis Major

Down
1. Castor
2. Betelgeuse
3. Taurus
4. Eridanus
6. Procyon
8. Pollux
9. Auriga
11. Canis Minor
12. Aldebaran
15. Rigel

The Fall Sky, page 126

Across
1. Fomalhaut
4. Mira
6. Andromeda
9. Pegasus
10. Aries
11. Delphinus
12. Cetus

Down
2. Hamal
3. Capricornus
5. Perseus
6. Aquarius
7. Pisces
8. Triangulum

The Summer Sky, page 127

Across
5. Vega
6. Ophiuchus
8. Libra
9. Antares
11. Cygnus
13. Serpens
14. Altair
15. Sagittarius
16. Corona Borealis

Down
1. Delphinus
2. Hercules
3. Aquila
4. Lyra
7. Scorpius
10. Sagitta
12. Deneb
14. Albireo

OVERHEAD PROJECTOR PANTY HOSE CONSTELLATION VIEWER

You will need a dark plastic panty hose container, ice pick, correcting fluid, alcohol burner, torch or sterno can and a white label. Remove top (smaller part) of the panty hose container for dome of viewer. Place on flat surface. Place dots of correcting fluid on dome to indicate stars in constellation or sky. Heat tip of ice pick. Gently press heated tip of ice pick through plastic dome at desired star locations. Place on overhead projector to project image on screen. Identify constellation. Place small label with name of constellation on lower edge of dome.

 TIP: Both parts of the panty hose container can be used for this activity. The shorter, smaller section is preferred, but the taller section also works well for this exercise.

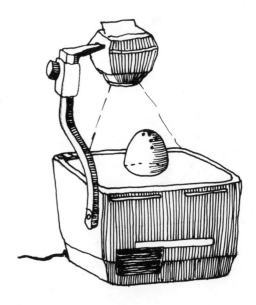

NIGHT SKY CONSTELLATION DOME
(STUDENT PAGE)

You will need a copy of this page, scissors, tape and pencil. With scissors, cut out the circle. Cut along the dotted line of the tape tab as far as the pole star, Polaris. Slide May section over tape tab to form concave sky dome. Tape the tape tab to underside of May section. Face north at 9:00 p.m. With thumb and forefinger grasp dome at the current month's position. Hold dome at arm's length slightly above eye level. The night sky will look like that found on the dome. Have students locate the following constellations: Big Dipper, Little Dipper, Draco, Cepheus, Cassiopeia and Camelopardalis.

TIP: After students have found the constellations, supply them with the answer key on page 131 to check their work. Students can also make the answer key dome page.

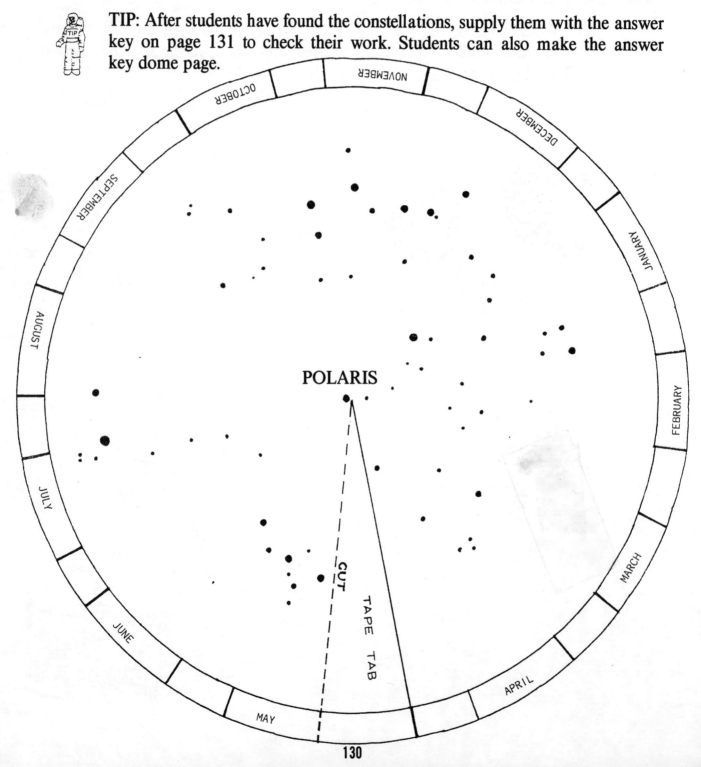

NIGHT SKY CONSTELLATION DOME
(TEACHER PAGE)

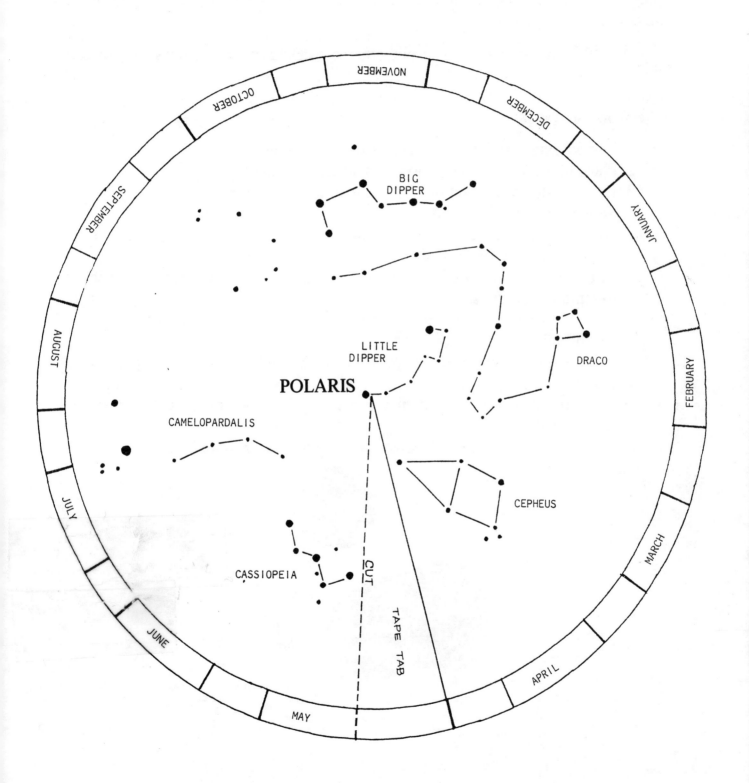

FILM CAN CONSTELLATION VIEWER

You will need a 35mm black film can without cover, a nail, ice pick, pushpin, corn skewer with one skewer cut off, and tape or glue. Have students cut out the constellation Cassiopeia circle below. Glue or tape to bottom of film can. With the sharp pointed object, have students punch holes through the paper and bottom of film can. Look through open end of film can toward the sky or a light to view the constellation Cassiopeia.

 TIP: Have students punch out other constellations in the ends of film cans.

Follow these steps:

1. Lay out wide masking tape sticky side up on table.
2. Place film can bottom end down on sticky masking tape.
3. Draw circle around can on sticky side of masking tape.
4. Remove film can from tape.
5. Draw dots to represent stars in a constellation of your choice inside circle on sticky side of masking tape.
6. Lift masking tape slightly from table. Punch holes through masking tape to represent the stars.
7. Place film can bottom end down over holes in circle on masking tape. Lift off table.
8. With a sharp pointed object, punch holes through the masking tape and bottom of film can at designated points. Separate film can from tape.
9. Look through open end of film can toward the sky or a light to view the constellation.
10. Enjoy your experience with constellations by making more of them.

CASSIOPEIA

DOUBLE FILM CAN CONSTELLATION VIEWER

You will need two 35mm black film cans with a lid, a pushpin, a piece of tape and scissors or drill. Cut or drill a hole the size of circle A in the bottom of film can A. Cut or drill a hole the size of circle B in the bottom of film can B. Place a piece of tape over the hole in the bottom of film can A. Punch small pinhole through the tape. Insert film can B bottom first into open end of film can A. With a pushpin, punch figure of constellation into film can cover B. Insert pushpin into rim where film cans A and B meet. Look at the sky or at a light through taped bottom of film can A. View constellation through cover on film can B.

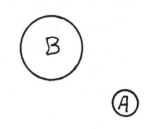

Actual sizes for holes in film cans

 TIP: Place film can lid A on film can B upright in line with the pushpin as the constellation appears in the sky. Thus, when the double film can constellation viewer is used, the pushpin should point upward and the constellation will appear exactly as it appears in the night sky.

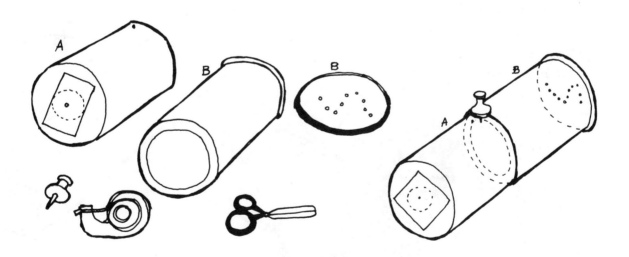

133

LONG TUBE CONSTELLATION VIEWER

You will need a copy of page 135, a potato chip can, piece of cardboard, hammer, nail, scissors, pins, stapler, white crayon or correcting fluid and black construction paper to make this handy long tube constellation viewer. Using a hammer and a nail, make a hole in the center of the metal end of the can. Staple page 135 to the black construction paper. Mount on cardboard with pins. With a straight pin, punch holes through white and black sheets of paper for each star in each constellation. Connect the dots on the black paper using white crayons or correcting fluid. Remove white copy page. Cut out six black circles. Place one circle at a time inside the lid of the can. Fasten lid. Have your students look through the hole in the metal end of the can to view constellation. Cover outside of the tube with black paper. With white crayon or correcting fluid, add constellation figures to outside of can. Have students identify each constellation.

 TIP: Save *white* copy page. Place on overhead projector for student to view all six constellations. This becomes a miniature planetarium. Your students can view each of the six constellations individually or all at one time using the punched white sheet placed on the overhead projector.

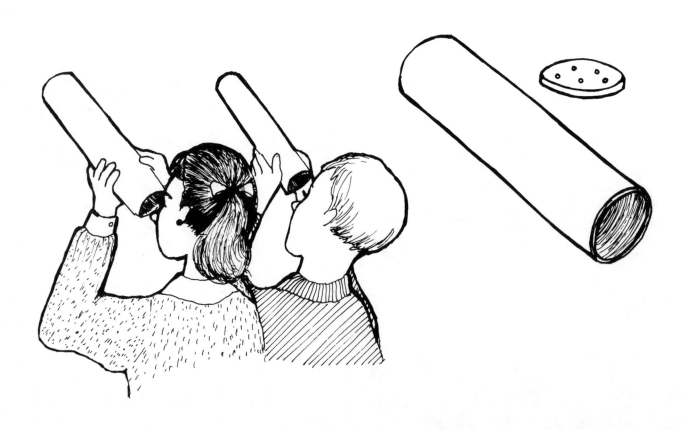

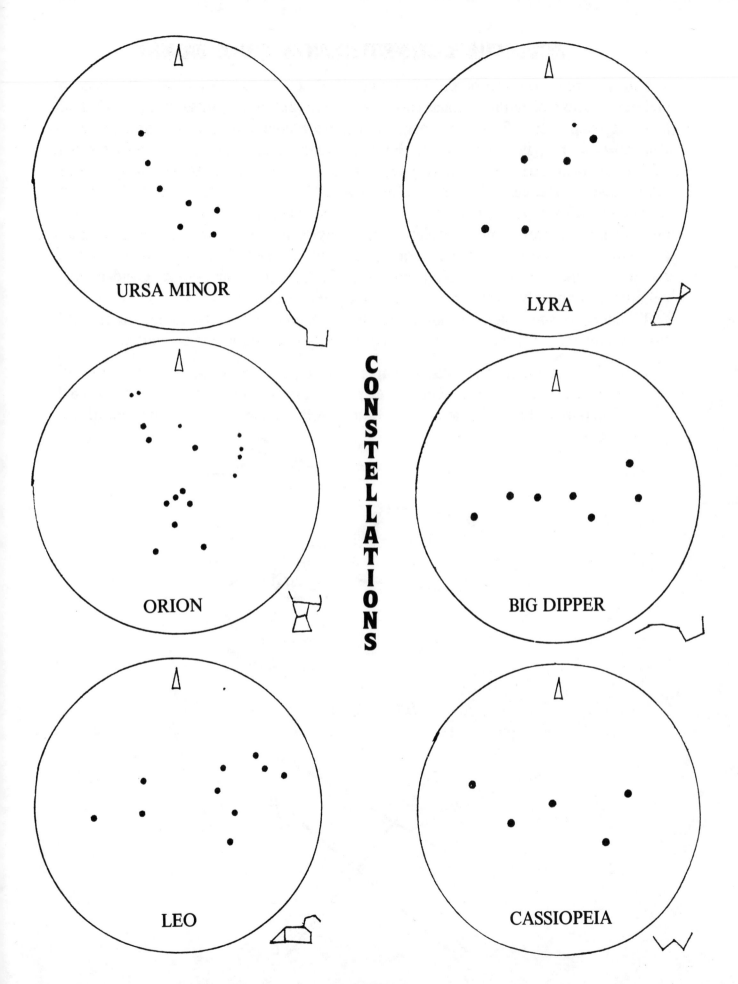

URSA MINOR

LYRA

ORION

BIG DIPPER

LEO

CASSIOPEIA

CONSTELLATIONS

ELECTRICAL CONSTELLATION QUIZ BOARD

You will need a copy of the next page, 8½″ x 11″ (22 cm x 28 cm) piece of tagboard (backs of writing tablets work well), aluminum foil, scissors, glue, ¾″ clear tape, paper punch, 1.5 volt dry cell, bulb, bulb holder and several wires. Tape or glue quiz board page to tagboard. Fold on dotted line. Punch holes A-E through both edges of folded page. Unfold page and lay flat. Punch holes 1-5 through single thick page near edge. With scissors, cut five 12″ x 1″ (30 cm x 2.5 cm) strips of aluminum foil for wires. Fold each wire in half lengthwise to make 12″ x ½″ (30 cm x 2.5 cm) wires. Connect holes A and 3 with aluminum foil. Cover aluminum foil with ¾″ (2 cm) clear tape. Proceed to connect holes B to 5, C to 4, D to 2 and E to 1. Be sure to cover each wire with ¾″ (2 cm) clear tape to avoid a short circuit. Set up quiz board tester so it looks like the one below.

Touch probes to matching holes to correctly match the constellation figure with the name of the constellation. If the light goes on, you have the correct match.

 TIP: Tape fold-over ends of paper fastener to ends of wires on probes. This prevents sharp ended wires from penetrating the aluminum foil within each matching hole. By doing this, your electrical constellation quiz board will last longer.

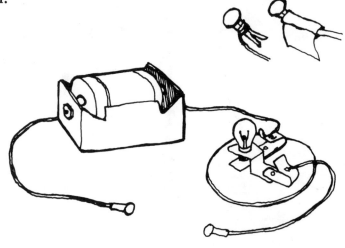

BACK SIDE

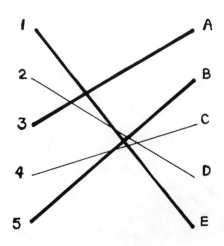

136

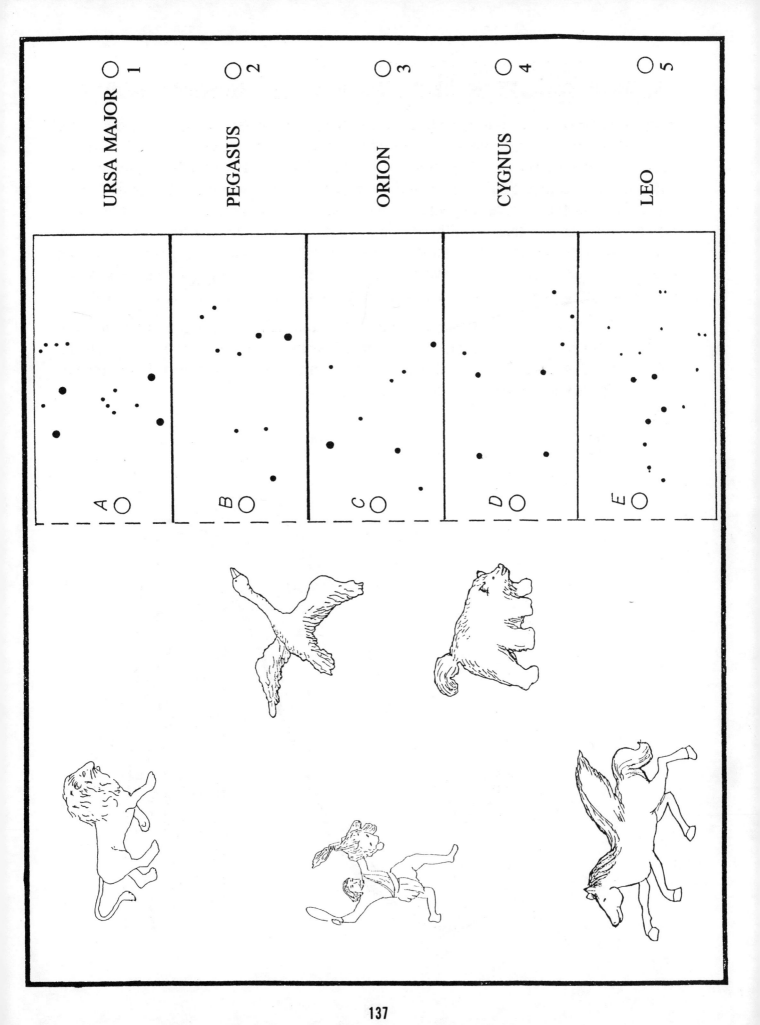

URSA MAJOR 〇 1

PEGASUS 〇 2

ORION 〇 3

CYGNUS 〇 4

LEO 〇 5

A 〇

B 〇

C 〇

D 〇

E 〇

SLIDER QUESTION AND ANSWER ASTRONOMY BOARD

You will need a copy of the slider frame master, scissors, oaktag, glue, tape and slider. Begin by making copies of the slider frame master (page 139) and slider A (page 140) for each student. Mount on oaktag. Cut out two windows and thumb notch in slider frame. Fold Tabs A and B on dotted lines towards back side of frame. Tape tabs together where they meet on the back of the slider frame. Insert slider A into slider frame. Read word(s) in window one and matching response in window two. Discuss responses. Have youngsters quiz each other. Then have students make their own sliders that feature science words or questions with matching responses on astronomy topics of their choice. Discuss the content of each newly created slider.

 TIP: Encourage students to make sliders that feature in-depth questions and answers. On the slider, have students position answer that will appear in window two, one space above or below window one so answer will not appear directly across from window one.

138

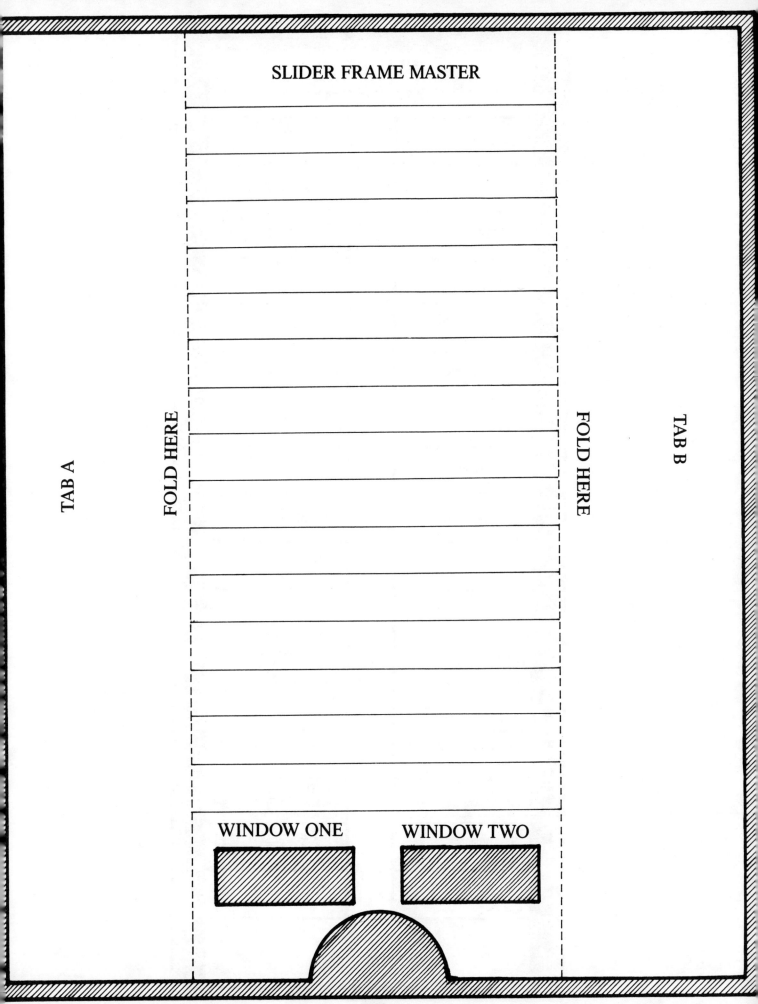

SLIDER FRAME MASTER

TAB A

FOLD HERE

FOLD HERE

TAB B

WINDOW ONE

WINDOW TWO

SLIDER FRAME MASTER

SLIDER A
ASTRONOMY

16. Light Year	16. The distance that light travels in one year in a vacuum
15. A.U.	15. Astronomical unit: the distance (93 million miles) from the earth to the sun
14. First day of summer in the United States	14. When the Northern Hemisphere is tilted toward the sun, usually June 21st
13. Earth's period of revolution around the sun	13. 365¼ days
12. Earth's period of rotation on its axis	12. One day
11. Moon's period of revolution around the earth	11. One month
10. Comet	10. Large, dirty ice ball or iceberg
9. Falling star	9. Rock burning up as it enters the earth's atmosphere
8. Smallest planet	8. Pluto
7. Planet most like the sun	7. Jupiter
6. Planet most like the earth	6. Mars
5. Number of stars in the Milky Way Galaxy	5. 100 billion (100,000,000,000)
4. Planet closest to the sun	4. Mercury
3. Brightest star in the night sky	3. Sirius
2. Astrology	2. The study of how things on Earth are related to the stars in the sky
1. Astronomy	1. The study of laws that govern the movements of all the stars

PULL

SPECTROSCOPE

You will need a shoe box, flat black paint, diffraction grating, tape, scissors, and two 2″ (5 cm) pieces of exposed 35mm film. Paint inside of box and underside of cover with flat black paint to reduce reflected light. Cut a 1″ (2.5 cm) square hole in the center of each end of the box. Tape 1.5 square inch (3 cm²) diffraction grating inside the box covering one of the holes. Cut a 2″ (5 cm) exposed film and tape over slit to cardboard mounting leaving a gap about the thickness of a note card between the two pieces of film. Tape mounting with attached film to end of shoe box. Fasten lid to the box with tape. Have youngsters look through diffraction grating end of shoe box to observe spectra of incandescent lights, fluorescent lights, street lights and neon lights. On a piece of paper, have youngsters color what they see inside the spectroscope.

 TIP: Thin slits in Pringle's cans and in various sizes of tubes also work well for this activity. Discuss various wavelengths found in the electromagnetic spectrum below. Then discuss what the words *Roy G. Biv* mean. (Colors of the spectrum: red, orange, yellow, green, blue, indigo and violet.)

TIP: Diffraction-grating material can be obtained from: Edmund Scientific Company, 101 E. Gloucester Pike, Barrington, NJ 08007.

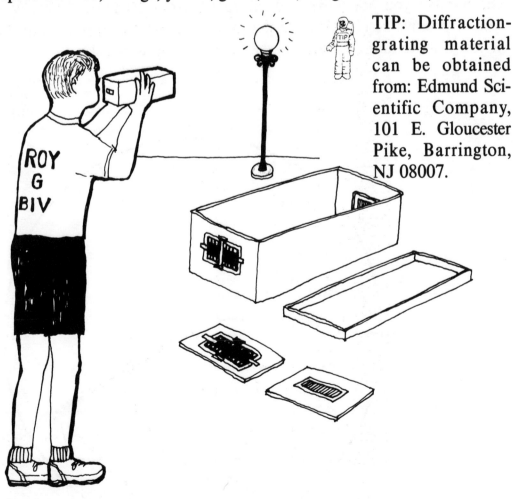

ELECTROMAGNETIC   SPECTRUM

Electric Power Waves	Radio & Television Waves	Infrared Waves	Visible Waves	Ultraviolet Waves	X – Rays	Gamma Rays	Cosmic Rays

BIG DIPPER TIME

"What time is it?" Naturally the answer to this question can easily be obtained by simply looking at your watch or any other nearby clock. But, I bet you have never realized that the answer can also be found in the stars!

Telling time by the stars has been a common practice for many ancient civilizations. It has only been since the development of mechanical devices that we moved away from using the stars. The process of telling time is very simple. With some practice and keen observations, you will be able to give the correct time within one-half hour.

Stand outside on any clear night. Locate the Big Dipper and the North Star, Polaris. Imagine that Polaris is at the center of a large clock and that the two pointer stars of the Big Dipper are the hour hand of the clock. An arrow drawn through the pointer stars directed away from Polaris will point to an hour of time on your imaginary clock. Read the time to the nearest hour. For a more accurate result, read the time to the nearest half-hour. To that time, add the number of months that have passed since the first of January. Do not forget to add any fraction of a month. Double the number you now have and subtract it from 16.25 or 40.25, whichever will give you a positive result. Your final answer will be the approximate time of night. So if you want to know the time of the evening, look to the sky.

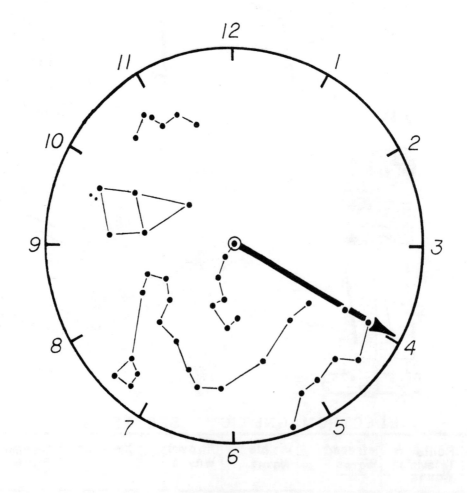

SUNDIAL

You will need a large piece of plywood or three sheets of single-layered cardboard, glued together; stick or dowel; clay; erasable marking pen; paper clips; and clear Con-Tact paper. Obtain a large sheet of plywood, triple-wall, or glue three sheets of single-layered cardboard together. Refrigerator boxes work well for this. Cover with clear Con-Tact paper. Cut a hole in the center of the sheet or put a ball of clay in the center. Insert dowel or stick into hole or clay so it's in a vertical position. With erasable pen, write *N, S, E* and *W* near four edges of cardboard. Go outside. Orient sundial with *S* facing south. At thirty-minute intervals, draw the stick's shadow on the cardboard. Draw lines using erasable felt-tipped pens. Mark the end of each shadow with a paper clip or pebble. Have students measure sun's shadow every thirty-minutes. Note direction (E, W, N, S) in which the shadow appears to travel. Note season of year and location of stick's shadow. Reuse sundial often by wiping off pen marks with damp cloth or paper towel. Then have students do research on Stonehenge.

TIP: **Caution students never to look directly at the sun for any reason.** Have younger students roll out adding machine tape the length of the stick's shadow. Record time of day on each ensuing strip of adding machine tape. Post on wall for all to see. Discuss the lengths of strips of adding machine tape for various times of the day. At which time of the day is the stick's shadow the longest? Shortest?

ANALEMMA

An analemma shows the position of the sun and its *declination* (latitude) every day of the year. You will need a copy of this page; tape or glue; scissors; tagboard; erasable pen and laminating machine, if available. Cut out rectangle below. Mount on tagboard. Laminate if possible.

Have students find the equator. Define *latitude* as the distance in degrees north or south of the equator. Have students locate Tropic of Cancer and Tropic of Capricorn. Point out that the sun appears at different heights in the sky at different latitudes. If page is laminated, have students circle September 23rd and March 21st with an erasable pen; otherwise mark on page. On these days, the sun at noon is directly overhead at the equator. Locate June 21st. The sun is located overhead at the Tropic of Cancer and thus is the longest day of the year in the Northern Hemisphere. Locate Tropic of Capricorn. The sun is directly overhead here on December 21st, the shortest day of the year for those in the Northern Hemisphere, the longest day for those in the Southern Hemisphere.

TIP: Place thin strip of magnetic tape on analemma. Cut out sun below. Place thin strip of magnetic tape on back of the sun. Move the sun around analemma each day to show the apparent position of the sun on that day of the year.

TIP: With a copying machine, enlarge the analemma and sun below. Mount on poster board. Attach magnetic tape to analemma and sun.

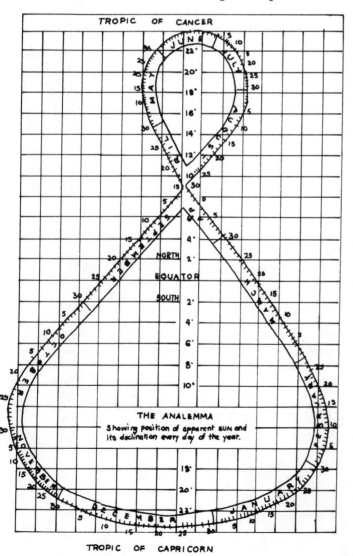

144

PIZZA WHEEL SOLAR SYSTEM

You will need some pizza wheels or circles of cardboard, string, pen, and paper punch. Obtain pizza wheels or cardboard for the sun and each planet. Label the larger circle the sun, the smaller circles the names of the planets. Punch nine holes around edge of sun, one hole per planet. Attach string from each planet to the sun. Identify two students per planet. Have students walk off appropriate distance with planet and string. After entire solar system has been set up and discussed, have youngsters wind string around each planet. Store model for future use.

TIP(S): (1) Write the names of the *moons* for each planet on additional pizza wheels. With colored stickers, color code moons to planets. Have students match moon to appropriate planet, (2) write pertinent information about each planet or moon on the reverse side of the cardboard, (3) use a hula hoop for the sun. Insert plastic rings on hula hoop, one for each planet. Attach string for planet to plastic ring so planets can be rotated around hula hoop. (4) Neptune, the farthest away planet from the sun until the year 1999, can be exchanged with Pluto in the model below.

145

MODEL SOLAR SYSTEM

You will need some paper; tagboard or cardboard; rulers; scissors; string; paper punch; wire and laminating machine, if available. Cut out a circle of tagboard for each planet according to size found on the next page. Label the sun and each planet. Laminate each. Punch hole in each planet and string on wire across classroom. Attach sun to wall at end of wire. Space out each planet according to scale based on the approximate distance of orbit from the sun. Use the chart on the following page.

 TIP: (1) The positions of Neptune and Pluto can be interchanged until the year 1999, as Neptune is the farthest away planet until that time. (2) Blow up balloons to simulate actual sizes of the planets. (3) Use solar system as a record keeping system of creative works. For example, each student has a clip that can be attached to the wire and moved along as each creative activity is completed.

SOLAR SYSTEM

SIZE (DIAMETER)

	IN	CM	MILES	KM
SUN	43	109	864,988	1,392,000
MERCURY	$\frac{5}{32}$	.4	3,032	4,880
VENUS	$\frac{6}{16}$	.9	7,519	12,100
EARTH	$\frac{7}{16}$	1.0	7,926	12,756
MOON	$\frac{1}{8}$	.3	2,141	3,446
MARS	$\frac{7}{32}$	.5	4,221	6,794
JUPITER	$4\frac{7}{16}$	11.2	88,984	143,200
SATURN	$3\frac{11}{16}$	9.4	74,568	120,000
URANUS	$1\frac{9}{16}$	4.0	31,940	51,400
NEPTUNE	$1\frac{1}{2}$	3.9	30,759	49,500
PLUTO	$\frac{1}{16}$	.2	1,864	3,000

DISTANCE OF ORBIT FROM SUN

IN	CM	MILES	KM	AU
—	—	—	—	—
$1\frac{5}{16}$	5.8	36,000,000	57,900,000	.4
$4\frac{1}{4}$	10.8	67,000,000	108,200,000	.7
6	15.0	93,000,000	149,600,000	1.0
6	15.0	93,000,000	149,600,000	1.0
9	22.9	140,000,000	227,900,000	1.5
31	78.0	480,000,000	778,300,000	5.2
56	143.0	890,000,000	1,427,000,000	9.5
113	288.0	1,800,000,000	2,871,000,000	19.2
177	451.0	2,800,000,000	4,497,100,000	30.0
233	593.0	3,700,000,000	5,913,500,000	39.5

POP CAN SOLAR SYSTEM

This activity helps you compare the various relative weights of an item on the nine planets and the moon. As future astronauts venture to the other bodies in our solar system they will experience different "pulls" of gravity. This change in the pull of gravity on the planets will result in a change in the astronaut's weight. On some planets they may weigh more than what they do on earth or they may even weigh less. For instance, an astronaut who weighs 180 pounds on Earth will weigh only 30 pounds on the moon. On Mars, the same astronaut will weigh approximately 72 pounds.

For this exercise, you will need ten empty pop cans, an indelible marker, a bag of plaster of Paris, some water and a scale. Mark each can with the name of one of the nine planets. Mark the last one the Moon. Fill the Jupiter can to the top with the plaster of Paris mixture. (Be sure you follow the instructions on how to mix the plaster of Paris.) Let the plaster in the Jupiter can harden. After the plaster in the Jupiter can has hardened, measure its mass. For purposes of mathematics, you should measure everything in grams.

To determine the correct amount of plaster to put in each of the remaining cans, multiply the mass of the Jupiter can by each of the following numbers:

Earth	.395
*Moon	.063
Mercury	.150
Venus	.359
Mars	.150
Saturn	.420
Uranus	.364
Neptune	.466
*Pluto	.019

Example: If the Jupiter can has a mass of 800 grams (.80 kg) then the earth can should be filled until its mass is 316 grams.

$$
\begin{array}{r}
800 \\
\times\ .395 \\
\hline
316 \text{ grams}
\end{array}
$$

Starting with the earth can, have each student hold the ten cans individually and compare what the earth can would weigh on each body in the solar system.

 TIP: Because the pull of gravity on Pluto is so small, use an empty can to represent the weight of Pluto.

TIP: Avoid putting plaster of Paris in a sink as it will clog the drain.

PIZZA WHEEL MOON PHASES WITH MATCHING MAGNETIC NAME CARDS

You will need some cardboard, scissors, paintbrush, black and white latex paint, note cards, pen and magnetic tape. Make eight equal-sized circles and one ring slightly larger than the circles. Paint white and black as shown below. Write the names of the moon phases on index cards. Laminate. Attach magnetic tape to the back of the moon phases, ring, and matching name cards so they will adhere to a metal cabinet or magnetic chalkboard. Each morning, have students encircle the correct phase of the moon with the ring. Record moon observations each day for at least one month noting any changes in size, shape and position of the moon.

 TIP: Instead of paint, use black and white Con-Tact paper to cover each of the eight moon phases.

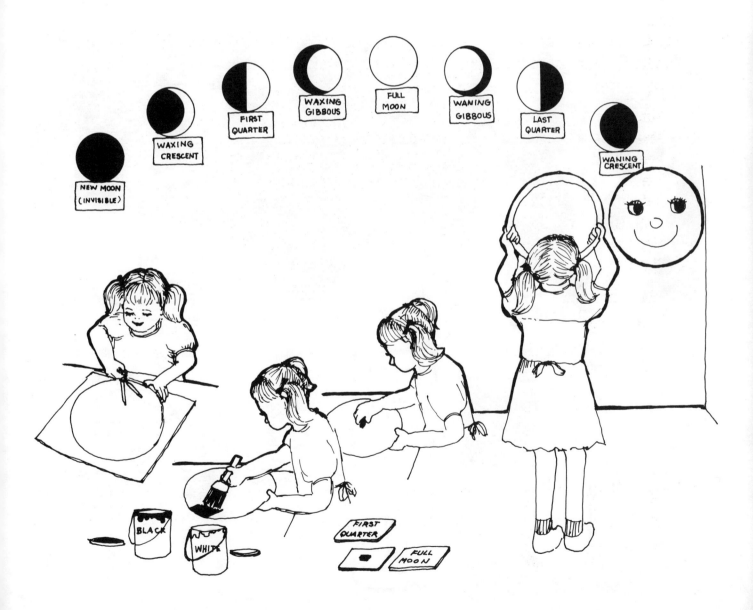

ASTROLABE

You will need a protractor or a half circle of scrap wood or stiff cardboard, a piece of string, a nut or washer, tape and a soda straw. Tape straw along edge of protractor or half circle of stiff cardboard. Hang piece of string with nut or washer attached, from the center of the protractor or cardboard. Mark number of degrees. Sight celestial body, like the moon, through the straw. Press string against the astrolabe. Read number of degrees the moon is above the horizon. (The horizon is an apparent line where the earth and the sky meet.) Be sure to subtract from 90° as you are using the protractor upside down. Have students observe the moon for one month. Carefully make sketches noting the moon's size, shape and position.

 TIP: Have students sight the North Star using their astrolabes. The North Star's altitude, the number of degrees above the horizon, will equal the students' *latitude*.

ASTROLABE

PROTRACTOR

STRAW

STRING

NUT

TAPE

REFLECTIONS

"We had the sky, up there, all speckled with stars, and we used to lay on our backs and look up at them, and discuss about whether they was made, or only just happened—Jim he allowed they was made, but I allowed they just happened—I judged it would have took too long to *make* so many. Jim said the moon could a *laid* them; well, that looked kind of reasonable, so I didn't say nothing against it, because I've seen a frog lay most as many, so of course it could be done."

Huck Finn, in
Mark Twain's *Huckleberry Finn* (1884)

MEET THE AUTHORS

Jerry DeBruin is a teacher at the University of Toledo in Toledo, Ohio. He is a member of the Department of Elementary and Early Childhood Education, and his specialty is science, although he truly enjoys all facets of education and life.

Jerry was born and raised on a farm in Wisconsin, and it was there that he nurtured his interest in science, the world around him and life in general. He has taught all grade levels in some capacity or another and currently spends a great deal of time in schools helping teachers and youngsters.

In addition to being the author of nineteen Good Apple books (some appear in the Smithsonian Institute in Washington, D.C.) and over 160 educational publications, Jerry is the recipient of many awards such as the 1984 Outstanding Teacher of the Year Award at the University of Toledo, the 1986 Martha Holden Jennings Outstanding Educator Award and the National Science Teachers Association 1986 Search for Excellence in Science Education Program Award.

Being a local, state, regional, national and international consultant in science education, Jerry's main interest in life is to develop in people a deep level of awareness and understanding of peaceful feelings toward themselves and others around the world. His works nurture this interest.

Peaceful Skies,

Jerry De Bruin

Don Murad has been a physics and astronomy teacher at St. Francis de Sales High School in Toledo, Ohio, for thirteen years. Born in Cleveland, Ohio, Don moved to Toledo in 1971 to attend the University of Toledo. There he majored in secondary education and physics receiving a Bachelor of Education degree in 1975 and a Masters of Education degree in 1980.

Don has been an avid amateur astronomer for over twenty years. He enjoys spending hours observing and photographing the night sky. His interest in astronomy has led to travels to various parts of the world to observe and photograph celestial events.

Don strongly believes in setting personal goals in all aspects of life and working hard to reach those goals.

Clear Skies,

Don Murad

AND ARTIST

Rochana Junkasem was born in Bangkok, Thailand. In 1971, she received her Bachelor of Architecture degree from Chulalongkorn University and taught there for six years before coming to the United States under a Fulbright Fellowship. Rochana believes that education is very important in life. Continuing her education in the United States, she received her Master of Fine Arts degree from Bowling Green State University in 1980 and her Ph.D. in Curriculum and Instruction from the University of Toledo in 1984. At present, she teaches art at the Toledo Museum of Art and Bowling Green City Schools. Rochana's main message to youngsters is that if people in countries throughout the world became one family, the world would be a better place in which to live.

Serene Sky,

Rochana Junkasem

ด้วยความปรารถนาดี

จาก

ดร. รจนา จันทร์เกษม